The Duel

The Duel

Giacomo Casanova

Translated by J.G. Nichols

ET REMOTISSIMA PROPE

100 PAGES

100 PAGES
Published by Hesperus Press Limited
4 Rickett Street, London SW6 1RU
www.hesperuspress.com

Il duello first published in Italian in 1780
This translation first published by Hesperus Press Limited, 2003

Introduction and English language translation © J.G. Nichols, 2003
Foreword © Tim Parks, 2003

Designed and typeset by Fraser Muggeridge
Printed in the United Arab Emirates by Oriental Press

ISBN: 1-84391-032-2

CONTENTS

FOREWORD

In an angry footnote to his *Discourse on the Customs of the Italians*, written in 1824, the philosopher-poet Giacomo Leopardi complains:

> 'No matter how remarkable a man may be, now matter how independent, how forthright, how stubborn in his behaviour and opinions and judgements of whatever kind, yet, if he live in society, his thoughts and actions are truly his own only to the smallest degree. In almost every way he is determined and modified by others, even those for whom he has little or no respect.'

Isn't this infuriating? No one could have been more stubbornly independent than Giacomo Casanova, more remarkable and resourceful, but *The Duel* is the story of how his apparently free spirit is fatally hijacked by the opinions of a resentful ballerina, the crass insults of a drunken Polish officer, and the absurdity of a society that demands that in certain circumstances a man behave in a manner at once suicidal and punishable by death.

I first came to Casanova's writing through W.G. Sebald who, in his novel *Vertigo*, refers at length to the Venetian writer's *History of my Flight from the Prison of the Republic of Venice*. Sebald's evident enthusiasm persuaded me to buy the book. It begins in Kafkaesque fashion. For no apparent reason, Casanova is arrested at dawn and imprisoned in a stifling, rat-infested cell beneath the roof of the Doges' Palace. Languishing here for months, he has no way of knowing whether he is to be released next week, next month, or never. He is afraid he will go mad. After a year of frustration and false starts, he dreams up the most daring and complicated of escapes – few works of fiction can compete – and as the book closes he is escaping north through the Alps to Austria and Munich.

How strange then, to open *The Duel* and find Casanova picking up his story with the regret that he ever bothered to leave his cell. It seems he was shortly to be released. He could have returned to his familiar life in Venice. For if a man is inevitably conditioned by those around him, better, Casanova feels, as do most Italians, if those people are his own people. Now he is an outlaw, liable to immediate arrest on return. Throughout *The Duel*, the author refers to himself in the third person as 'the Venetian', as if, being exiled, he had somehow been estranged from himself, yet is still most determined by the city and culture that gave him birth.

Casanova may regret escape and exile but the reader does not. *The Duel* proceeds with a splendidly cheeky account of the adventurer's travels through the capitals of Northern Europe. Never have so many courts and kings been so quickly caricatured and dismissed. Expelled from his own society, the Venetian is free to see every other for what it is: absurd. Again and again the long, sonorous sentences, the product, it would seem, of a lofty civilisation, end in a lash of corrosive wit. Again and again the object of ridicule is a figure of authority, a king, even the Pope. These are only the 1760s, but the Revolution is already in the air. How ridiculous that a queen who casually remarks that chicken fricassee is the best dish in the world starts a whole country eating chicken fricassee and swearing blind that it is indeed the best dish in the world. Just because she is the queen! How crazy that people respect me because I wear a fancy medal awarded to me for no other reason than that I once kissed the holy pontiff's sacred feet. Aren't people stupid? Convinced of his superiority, our Venetian toes society's line, eating up court freebies beside princes and ladies, perfectly aware that the emperor has no clothes, but with no intention at all of 'undeceiving the deceived'. Absurdity is fun.

Then, in Warsaw, an Italian ballerina comes to town. Casanova admires her, but he admires another just as much. Actually, and rather out of character, he isn't paying a great deal of attention. Is this something to do with a certain 'medicine', he is taking? The dancer, no doubt aware of his reputation, is angry. Meanwhile, one of her more attentive admirers is General Branicki, a man whom Casanova mocks as having 'learnt to shed the blood of his enemies without hating them, to take vengeance without any anger, to kill without discourtesy, to prefer honour, which is an imaginary good, to life, which is the only real good which men have'.

Fatal words. Fatal pride. All too soon, it will be the insulted Venetian who will be risking his life as he challenges this pompous Pole to a duel for the sake of honour.

The remarkable thing about Giacomo Casanova is that not only did he have a bewilderingly eventful life, not only was he a thinker of wide reading and great shrewdness, but he also knew how to tell a tale as well as the cleverest of novelists, knew, above all, how to wring out of it the maximum tension and irony. Both the Venetian and the reader have been beautifully set up in the opening pages of this book. We thought we had seen through all society's self-regarding theatre. We thought we were immune. Until, in the space of a few lines, here we are enthralled by one of the most grotesque and artificial rituals ever devised: two men back to back in the snow, loaded pistols in their hands, everything at stake, all because of a woman now entirely for-gotten and indeed never again mentioned throughout the book.

Public opinion may be a matter of no substance, observed Schopenhauer, yet if everybody else foolishly pays attention to it, then you will have to do likewise. For it conditions your whole existence. Especially if you depend on your charm and social graces to scrounge a living through the courts of Europe. Such, more or less, is the Venetian's reasoning when he decides to challenge the man who has insulted him. A loss of reputation would be a loss of earning power. Yet as the two combatants warm to their madness, as they become extravagantly deferential to each other in a delirium of mutual admiration – what crazy courage we are showing! – one can't help feeling that there is more to the ritual of the duel than our hero supposes.

More than a hundred years after Casanova, discussing *The Varieties of Religious Experience*, the psychologist William James suggested that risking one's life could give you a sense of sacred transport. He quotes a certain General Skobelev: '…a meeting of man to man, a duel, a danger into which I can throw myself headforemost, attracts me, moves me, intoxicates me. I am crazy for it, I love it, I adore it. I run after danger as one runs after women…'

Well, who ran after women more than Giacomo Casanova? Here is the key. The Venetian may merely be responding to society's absurd notions of honour when he challenges his opponent. He hadn't planned to do this. It is a loss of independence. But once he engages, the absurd duel gives this jaded, disillusioned man a sense of meaning that even young ballerinas are no longer capable of providing. Curiously, it also forges a new and very intimate society: between the Venetian and his opponent, and between this eighteenth-century adventurer and ourselves. We all share the disturbing awareness that, precisely because it is our most precious asset, there comes a time when life must be risked.

– Tim Parks, 2003

INTRODUCTION

Casanova – the proverbial assiduous lover or lecher, according to one's viewpoint – is seen in this volume rather as an adventurer, man-about-many-towns, indefatigable name-dropper, crack shot, amateur theologian, skilled diplomat with an admirable ability to think on his feet, smooth talker, and (what makes us aware of all these qualities) a fine writer. The events leading up to the duel, the fight itself, and the even more bizarre events which follow it, are all presented in a lively, dramatic way. There is no doubt that we have here that often-despised, but always compelling, thing – 'a rattling good yarn'. And there is much more to it than that. What happens, what is said, and the reactions of the participants to what happens and what is said, all occur against a background of Enlightenment ideas, of generally accepted notions of good and bad behaviour, which are in many ways alien to us now, and all the more interesting for that.

It is not surprising that duelling has so often furnished material for literature: there are two elements in it whose combination is irresistibly dramatic – absurdity and idealism (absurdity that men are willing to kill or be killed sometimes apparently out of mere pique, and idealism in that there are certain standards of behaviour involved, and anyway no one can fail to admire, at least a little, the apparent indifference to wounds or death). So we find ourselves amused almost to laughter at times, and frequently full of admiration for a cool mind, a cool hand, a cool eye, and considerable cool cheek.

Moreover, serious social issues are involved in duelling. It could be, as Francis Bacon said of revenge in general, 'a kind of wild justice' in societies where nothing like our modern systems of law-enforcement and justice (however faulty they may be) existed. It could also be a more or less controlled outlet for a violence that might otherwise express itself in even more disruptive ways. Then it had other functions, to which we may well be inclined to be less sympathetic. It was one way of maintaining an existing hierarchical social order, since it emphasised class divisions: duelling was a 'gentlemanly' thing, which the lower orders and women would occasionally imitate, but could never really rise to with the same élan. Duelling was, for hundreds of years, in an equivocal position – both socially and religiously. The law of the land normally condemned it; and yet governments were well aware that, both for national defence and for the preservation of social order, they had to rely upon soldiers (usually the most enthusiastic duellists) who prized a good fight more than their own lives; and so duelling was often winked at by the powers that be. If surviving duellists had always been treated as murderers and executed, there would have been a chronic shortage of officers all over Europe. Theologically the problem was a simpler, but a no less recalcitrant one. For hundreds of years the Church had opposed those ancestors of the duel, trial by combat and tournaments, without being able to get rid of them, and it disapproved of the formal duelling of the eighteenth century, with the same lack of success. This was not simply a matter of condemning a sin which continued to be committed: duelling was at times so much a part of upper-class mores as to present itself almost as an alternative system of belief. Yet the duellists were usually Christians ('more or less', as Casanova says of himself and his opponent), and so there was a strange co-existence of incompatibles.

All those features of duelling – and many more – lie behind Casanova's accounts, where they are not stated as general-isations, but tacitly understood; and they are seen to be all the more powerful, and powerfully conveyed by the writing, because the understanding is tacit.

Perhaps surprisingly, some of those practical features of duelling which are familiar from literature and drama, and which derive from the many manuals of DIY duelling which were produced in the seventeenth and eighteenth centuries, are absent from this duel. I mean such apparently important details as the use of seconds to arrange the affair and see that it is carried out fairly, lending also an atmosphere of courtesy and calm to a dangerous situation; the right of the man who is challenged to choose weapons; the decision as to how far apart the combatants should stand (which in this instance appears to be determined by the space that happens to be available!); the signal upon which firing should begin; and the point at which the duel may be regarded as over. This comparative lack of formality means that Casanova is in greater danger after the duel than before, but it also means that he is able to make one or two remarks, immediately before the duel, which have a great effect on its outcome. This neglect of many features of a standard, and sensible, procedure gives a greater air of vraisemblance to the whole event, and also reveals many of the assumptions behind the fight. There is a clash between Enlightenment formality and perennial human barbarism. Branicki's over-enthusiastic friend, Biszewski, who is anxious above all to kill *someone*, is duly punished, but he is clearly representative of a general reaction to the duel.

That there is a tacit understanding of what is involved is revealed in many ways. Both duellists bare their breasts: despite the professions of courtesy on both sides, each needs to be sure that no armour is worn under the clothes. This action of theirs shows also that it is taken for granted that each will aim at the other's chest, a fact of which the laterally thinking Casanova takes full advantage. Again, the guns have to be loaded on the spot, with the added condition of 'You load and I choose.' The episode which is most revelatory, however, is the conversation between Branicki and Casanova in which they arrange the duel, a conversation that in the longer, Italian version, is given in direct speech and set out as a play. This is in fact another duel, a verbal one this time, where both men are firing shots – trying to get the edge, psychologically as well as practically, on the other – and where not what is said, but what is understood, matters the most. Just one instance is Branicki's repeated complaint that he does not *know* Casanova; this has several implications. One, which becomes clearer in the course of the conversation, is that he is afraid that Casanova may be a fencing-master, and therefore have an unfair advantage with swords. (A strange thing when one considers that a duel is nothing if not a trial of skill, and an even more interesting thing when one learns later that Branicki is an exceptionally good shot.) Another implication, which only becomes clear after the fight, with several indications from other people, is that Branicki is not very happy about fighting someone who is beneath him socially.

In these accounts there is also much of interest which is not directly, if at all, concerned with duelling. Casanova is generous with advice for other chancers to profit by: we learn how, and how not, to make a fortune in Russia, for instance. And he is most helpful in setting an example for other adventurers to follow. We see his quick-wittedness and ready speech, his ability to maintain an apparent geniality, and also – although this can be much harder to pinpoint – his sense of humour. This comes out in his comments on his one decoration, the Roman order of knighthood. He is obviously pleased with it, and tells us the exact way in which he wears it, but he says also that it is 'a respectable decoration which impresses fools', and he sells it when he is short of cash. This is perhaps cynical enough; but what are we to think when he tells us that he had been 'disgusted with it for a long time, because he had seen several charlatans with the same decoration'? Comic in a similar way is the contrast he draws between the religious preparations made by Branicki and those made by himself before the duel. In this comparison Casanova comes off better, of course, as he always does, at least morally (if that is the right word), and in his own opinion; but one feels that the writer himself has something of the same amused attitude to these 'religious' devices as his reader inevitably has.

The inclusion in this volume of a second account of the duel – originally in French and drawn from Casanova's lengthy memoirs written towards the end of his life – is amply justified by the differences – of approach, detail, and emphasis – between the two accounts. In a strange way this adds to the impression of truth, since this is exactly, or rather inexactly, how anyone would remember the events of many years earlier and would adjust his telling of the anecdote. The first account, however, the Italian one, is the more impressive. For instance, the pre-duel dialogue between Branicki and Casanova is more summarily, and less effectively, dealt with in the French. But the greatest difference (a good indication of Casanova's skill as a writer) is that he avails himself in the first account of a device which he obviously could not use in the second – he writes in the third person, referring to himself throughout merely as 'the Venetian'. That this suggests a lack of bias in the account and a more consciously literary style is only the most obvious reason for its use. A more subtle reason is that it emphasises

Casanova's status as an outsider in Warsaw, a status that influences almost everything that happens. In their pre-duel dialogue Branicki says, 'I am aware of the tricks your nation gets up to.' This distrust of the foreigner is the cause of much of the unfair treatment of Casanova after the duel. And, as we are gradually made aware, the distrust is well-deserved. Indeed, Branicki's problem is that ultimately he is not sufficiently aware of the tricks which this one Italian gets up to.

Casanova's reputation in England is so firmly based on his amorous exploits that 'Casanova' is a label frequently applied to womanisers in everyday speech. It is refreshing to see here another, and more versatile, Casanova – the insouciant and engaging risk-taker. There is a caveat to be entered. I am writing of Casanova's accounts as literature, and ignoring the question of their veracity. This is simply because a discussion of that question would not only take me further than I wish to go, but further than I have the knowledge to go. In anything that purports to be history, the truth does matter; but we can here enjoy a well-written 'history' without worrying about its truth.

– *J.G. Nichols, 2003*

Note on the Text:
This translation of *The Duel* is based on the text included in Giacomo Casanova, *Fuga dai Piombi*, Rizzoli, Superbur Classici, 2002. The extract from Casanova's *Memoirs* is taken from Jacques Casanova de Seingalt, Vénitien, *Histoire de ma vie*, Édition intégrale, Tome Cinq (Vol. 10, chapter 8), F.A. Brockhaus, Wiesbaden, Librairie Plon Paris, 1961.

Polish names, often misspelt by Casanova, have here been corrected.

The Duel

An incident from the life
of the Venetian, G.C.

... animum rege; qui nisi paret
imperat; hunc frenis, hunc tu compesce catena.[1]

(Horace, *Epistles* I, 2, 62–3)

A man born in Venice to poor parents, without worldly goods and without any of those titles which in cities distinguish the families of note from common people, but, by the grace of God, brought up like one destined for something different from the trades followed by the populace, had the misfortune at the age of twenty-seven to fall foul of the government, and at the age of twenty-eight was lucky enough to escape from the sacred hands of that justice whose punishment he was unwilling to bear. That criminal is indeed fortunate who can tranquilly suffer the penalty which he deserves, waiting with patient resignation for it to end; that criminal is unfortunate who, after having erred, does not have the courage to make up for his faults and blot them out by due submission to his sentence. This Venetian was an impatient man; he fled, although he knew that by taking to flight he was endangering his life, something which he had no use for without his liberty. On the other hand, perhaps he did not think about it so much, but merely fled, as the lowest animals do, in simple obedience to the voice of nature. If the rulers, whose chastisement he was fleeing, had wanted to, they could of course have had him arrested during his flight, but they did not bother to, with the result that this ill-advised young man found out by experience that in his desire for liberty a man often exposes himself to vicissitudes which are much more cruel than short-lived slavery. An escaped prisoner never arouses in the minds of those who have condemned him any feeling of anger, but of pity rather, since by fleeing he blindly augments his own ills, renounces the benefits of his restoration to his homeland, and remains a criminal, just as he was before he started to expiate his crime.

In short, this Venetian, overcome by his youthful ardour, left the State by the longest route, since he knew that the shorter route is usually fatal to those in flight, and went to Munich, where he remained for one month in order to regain his health and to provide himself with money and honest attendants; and then, after crossing through Swabia, Alsace, Lorraine, and Champagne, he reached Versailles on the fifth of January in the year 1757, half an hour before the fanatic Damiens stabbed King Louis XV of happy memory.[2]

This man, who had by force of circumstances become an adventurer – for such anyone must be who is not rich and who goes through the world disgraced in his own country – had in Paris some extraordinary strokes of luck, which he abused. He passed into Holland, where he brought to a successful conclusion some business which produced a considerable sum of money, which he used up; and he went to England, where an ill-conceived passion almost made him lose his mind and his life. He left England in 1764, and through French Flanders he went into the Austrian Low Countries, passed over the Rhine, and through Wesel entered Westphalia. He went rapidly through the lands of Hanover and Brunswick, and via Magdeburg he reached Berlin, the capital of Brandenburg. In the two months he remained there – during which he had two audiences with King Frederick (a favour which His Majesty grants readily to all those foreigners who ask for it in writing) – he realised that serving that King gave no hopes of making a fortune. So he left Brandenburg with one servant and a man from Lorraine, an expert mathematician, whom he took with him as a secretary: since he intended to go and seek his fortune in Russia, he needed such a man. He stayed a few days in Danzig, a few in Königsberg, the capital of ducal Russia, and skirting the coast of the Baltic Sea he arrived at Mitau, capital of Courland[3], where he spent a month being well entertained by the illustrious Duke Johann Ernst Biron, at whose expense he inspected all the iron mines in the Duchy. He then left with a generous payment for having suggested to the Duke, and demonstrated the means of arranging, some useful improvements in the mines. Leaving Courland, he stayed a short while in Livonia, went rapidly through Karelia and Estonia and all those provinces, and came to Ingria, and then St Petersburg, where he would have found the fortune that he desired if he had gone there by invitation. No one should hope to make his fortune in Russia who goes there out of mere curiosity. 'What has he come here to do?' is a sentence which they all utter and they all repeat: he only is certain of being employed and given a fat salary who arrives at that Court after having had the skill to introduce himself in some European court to the Russian ambassador, who, if he becomes persuaded of that person's merit, informs the Empress, who gives the order to send him to her, paying the expenses of his journey. Such a person cannot fail to succeed, because no one would be able to say that money has been thrown away on the travel expenses of someone with no ability; this would mean that the minister who proposed him had been deceived, something that certainly could not happen, because ministers understand men very well. Ultimately the only man who does not have, and cannot have, any merit is the good man who goes there at his own expense. Let this be a warning to those of my readers who are considering going there uninvited in the hope of becoming rich in the imperial service.

Nevertheless our Venetian did not waste his time, since it was always his habit to be employed in some way or other. But he did not make his fortune. And so, at the end of a year, no better provided than he usually was, except for letters of exchange with good recommendations, he went to Warsaw.

He left St Petersburg in his carriage drawn by six post-horses, and with two servants, but with so little money that, when in a wood in Ingria he came upon Maestro Galuppi, known as Buranello[4], who was going there at the Czarina's behest, his purse was already empty. Despite that, he covered the nine hundred miles, which was how far it was to the capital of Poland, successfully. In that land he who has the air of needing nothing can easily make money, and it is not difficult there to have that air, just as it is most difficult to have it in Italy, where there is no one who supposes that a purse is full of gold until he has first seen it open. *Italiam! Italiam!*

The Venetian was very well-received in Warsaw. Prince Adam Czartoryski, to whom he introduced himself with a strong letter of recommendation, introduced him to his father, the Prince Palatine of Russia, to his uncle, the Grand Chancellor of Lithuania and a very learned jurisconsult, and to all the great ones of the kingdom who were there at Court. He was introduced by no other name than the one which he took from his humble birth, and his situation could not have been unknown to the Poles, since many of those great ones had seen him fourteen years previously in Dresden, where he had served King Augustus III with his pen, and where his mother, brothers, brothers-in-law, and nephews had been. The mendacious gentlemen of the press should hold their tongues. The poor wretches, however, do deserve some sympathy, since lying articles, particularly when they are slanderous, make their papers more fashionable than true accounts do. The only foreign addition which decorated the exterior of the not badly set-up figure of the Venetian was the Roman Order of Knighthood, rather the worse for wear, which he wore on a bright red ribbon hanging round his neck *en sautoir*, as the monsignors wear their crosses. He had received that Order from Pope Clement XIII of happy memory, when he had the good fortune to kiss his sacred foot in Rome in the year 1760. An Order of Knighthood, of whatever kind, provided it glitters, is a great help to a man who, when he is travelling, has occasion to appear for the first time in a different city almost every month; it is an ornament, a respectable decoration which impresses fools, and so it is necessary, since the world is full of fools, and they are all inclined to evil; therefore, when a beautiful Order of Knighthood can calm them down and make them ecstatic, confused, and respectful, it is well to flaunt it. The Venetian stopped wearing this Order in the year 1770 in Pisa where, finding himself in need of cash, he sold his cross, which was adorned with diamonds and rubies: he had been disgusted with it for a long time because he had seen several charlatans with the same decoration.

So, eight days after he arrived in Warsaw he had the honour to dine at the home of Prince Adam Czartoryski with that monarch of whom all Europe was talking, and whom he ardently longed to meet. At the round table, at which eight people were seated, everyone was eating a little or a great deal, except the King and the Venetian, since they were talking all the time both about Russia, which the monarch knew well, and about Italy, which he, although he was very curious about it, had never seen. Despite that, many people in Rome, in Naples, in Florence, in Milan have told me that they had entertained him in their homes; and I let them talk like this, and believe what they were saying, since in this world a man runs into great danger if he undertakes the difficult task of disillusioning those who are deceived.

After that dinner the Venetian spent all the remainder of that year and part of the following year paying homage to His Majesty, to those princes and those rich prelates, since he was always invited to all the glittering festivities which were held at Court and in the magnificent houses of the upper classes, and particularly in those of the *family* (as the famous house of Czartoryski was pre-eminently known) where true magnificence, far superior to that of the Court, reigned.

At that time there came to Warsaw a Venetian ballerina who with her grace and her charms captivated the minds of many, and among them that of the Grand Butler to the Crown, Ksawery Branicki. This gentleman, who today is a great general, was then in the prime of his life, a fine man, who, being inclined from his adolescence to the profession of arms, had served France for six years. There he had learnt to shed the blood of his enemies without hating them, to take vengeance without any anger, to kill without discourtesy, to prefer honour, which is an imaginary good, to life, which is the only real good men have. The office of the Equestrian Order of Grand Podstoli to the Crown (*podstoli* is a word which signifies butler) he had obtained from King Augustus III; he was decorated with the famous Order of the White Eagle; and he was returning at that time from the Court in Berlin to which he had been accredited by the new King, his friend, to perform a certain *secret* commission known to everyone. He was this King's favourite, and to him he afterwards owed his good fortune, for he was overwhelmed with favours. It is true too that he had earned his great rise in favour by his own valour in war, by his loyal companionship some years before Augustus had been elected King, when Augustus had been at the Court of St Petersburg, where he became an admirer of the eminent qualities, the spirit, and the beauty of the Grand Duchess of Muscovy, now the most glorious Empress. This knight was truly worthy of the predilection of his friend the King, since, just as he had been when they were equals, so when the other arrived at the splendour of the throne, he was the ever ready and almost blind executor of his orders on every occasion, and not with any less fervour when it was a matter of exposing himself by his service to mortal danger. He was that bold man who fought and made the whole Polish nation his enemy, beginning with that considerable party of malcontents who took to arms when the Diet of Convocation decided to place the royal diadem on the head of Stanislaus, now regnant, whom he adored. Towards the middle of the year 1766 the King conferred on him the very useful title of Lowczyc, or Grand Chasseur to the Crown, while he lay wounded by that dangerous pistol-shot which the Venetian gave him in the duel of which we are about to speak. To obtain that title, he forewent that of Grand Butler which, although it was two grades superior to the new title, was not lucrative: having money is something which many people prefer to any other kind of superiority.

The Venetian ballerina had no need of the protection of Branicki, Podstoli to the Crown, to make people respect her, because everyone loved her and she enjoyed also other more conspicuous protection; but the favour of the bold and brave Podstoli, a resolute knight who was not easy to get to know, augmented her reputation, and perhaps restrained those who, in theatrical factions that are at odds with each other, sometimes occasion the virtuous no little disgust.

The Venetian was by taste and out of a sense of duty a friend of the Venetian ballerina, but he had not, by ap-plauding her dancing, become hostile to that of another prima ballerina, whom he was friends with before the Venetian ballerina arrived at the Court of Warsaw. She bore this with bad grace. She thought that she could not quietly allow her only compatriot in Warsaw to be one of those who applauded her rival rather than simply one of her own supporters. A competitive woman of the theatre is so anxious for victory that she is the declared enemy of all those who do not lend a hand to subjugate whoever is in competition with her, and to enable her to triumph. This is how all theatrical heroines think: dominated by ambition and envy, they cannot pardon those who support their competitor, and there is no favour with which they are not ready to reward anyone who manages to escape from the other's fetters, if he can be supposed to contribute much to swinging the balance in their favour.

She had often complained to her Podstoli, who was then at the head of her faction, of the Venetian's ingratitude, but he did not know what to do; the only promise he made her was that, if the occasion presented itself, he would know how to humiliate him in the same way as in the past he had humiliated another who had not automatically felt able to side with her. The occasion, although it had to be dragged in by the scruff of its neck, was not long in presenting itself.

The 4th of March, St Casimir's Day, was celebrated by a fête at Court, because Casimir was the name of the Prince Grand Chamberlain, the King's brother. After the meal His Majesty told the Venetian that he would be glad to hear what he thought of the Polish theatre, since that day for the first time there was to be a performance on the Warsaw stage with Polish actors. The Venetian promised the King that he would be among the spectators, but begged him not to require his opinion, since he did not understand that language at all. The monarch smiled, which sufficed to show that the Venetian had received a great honour in that august assembly. When monarchs are being courted in public, in the crowded assembly of their ministers, of ambassadors, and of foreigners, they take care to direct some question or other to all those whom they wish to assure that their presence has been noted. Hence they have to think of some question which can be put to this person, or to that one, of those whom they wish to honour with conversation that will not be open to serious reflection, not equivocal, not such that the person questioned can reply that he does not know. Above all, monarchs speak straightforwardly and precisely, since it must never happen that the person, who is summoned by the royal voice to speak, has to reply: 'Sire, I do not understand what Your Majesty has said to me.' This reply would cause the assembly to laugh, because the idea it presents is absurd: either a king who was not understood because he did not know how to express himself, or a courtier who does not understand a king when he speaks. If it does happen that a courtier has not understood, either he lowers his head as a sign of his gratitude, or says whatever comes into his mind; whether it is to the point or not, it is always acceptable.

So the words that a sovereign says to anyone in public must be mere platitudes; but he must say something; if he does not, the matter is noticed, and the following morning the whole city knows that so-and-so is out of favour at Court, because at dinner the King did not address him. These trifles are very well-known to all sovereigns, in fact they make up one of the most important articles of their catechism, because even their slightest gesture is carefully examined by the Argus-eyed onlookers; and their words, however little they are susceptible of such treatment, are subject to a hundred different interpretations.

In the year 1750 I found myself at Fontainebleau in the company of those present at dinner with the Queen of France, or rather (to put it better) of those watching her eat. The silence was profound. The Queen, alone at table, looked only at the food which was put in front of her by her ladies-in-waiting. Then, having tasted one dish and wanting to indicate that she wished for a second helping, she raised her head majestically and, slowly turning her head to accompany her eyes – in contrast to certain injudicious gentlemen of our country, who, since they only turn their eyes and not their heads, look as though they are obsessed – she scanned the whole circle in an instant, then stopped at one gentleman, the greatest of all, and perhaps the only one to whom it suited her to do so much honour, and said to him in clear voice: '*Je crois, Monsieur de Lœvendal, que rien n'est meilleur d'une fricassée de poulets.*' ['I think, Monsieur de Lœvendal, that there is nothing better than a chicken fricassee.'] He (having already advanced three paces as soon as he heard the Queen pronounce his name) replied in a humble voice, seriously and gazing at her fixedly, but with his head lowered: '*Je suis de cet avis là, Madame.*' ['I am of that opinion, Madame.'] Having said this, he returned to where he had been before, keeping himself bowed and walking backwards on the tips of his toes, and the meal finished without another word being spoken.

I was beside myself. I stared at that great man, whom previously I had known only by name as the famous conqueror of Berg-op-Zoom, and I could not conceive how he had been able to keep a straight face – he, a marshal of France – at that remark, suitable for a cook, with which the Queen had deigned to address him, and to which he had replied in the same serious tone and with the same gravity with which, in a council of war, he would have advised the death of a guilty officer. The more I thought about it the harder I found it to repress the burst of laughter which was choking me. Woe betide me if I had not managed to repress it! They would have taken me for a downright madman, and God knows what would have happened to me. From that day onwards, that is for the whole month I spent at Fontainebleau, every day in every house where I dined, I found chicken fricassee. Cooks of both sexes were preparing it in competition with each other, and maintaining that the Queen had spoken truly, but that it was also true that in the whole French cuisine there was no dish more difficult to prepare. And I could never understand how that dish could in fact be so difficult, when I found it everywhere and everywhere equally perfect. But I restrained myself from expressing this thought because, now that the Queen had composed a eulogy to it, they would have booed me. I was firmly of the opinion that it was only the Queen's cook who could boast of preparing it to perfection.

Those words which on that day the King of Poland said to the Venetian, because he did not know what else to say to him, were the cause of the duel, because if the King had not so commanded him, it is certain that he would never have gone to be bored by the Polish stage. He went there, and after the first dance he noticed, as he stood behind the King's chair in the side-box, that His Majesty had clapped the ballerina Teresa Casacci. And so it occurred to him to go behind the scenes to compliment her, since on that day the King had not been generous with his applause to anyone else. On his way he went to pay a visit first to the Venetian ballerina in her dressing-room, where she was at her dressing-table preparing for the second dance. But he had hardly entered when the Podstoli appeared in front of him with a very dark look on his face. The Venetian, seeing him appear accompanied by Biszewski dressed in the Polish fashion as a lieutenant-colonel of his regiment, went away after bowing to them very politely. Those gallant courtiers beyond the mountains who make courtesy visits in their dressing-rooms to would-be virtuous ladies, are in the habit of going away when another visitor arrives, which is regarded as good manners since it is intended to please both parties, and the tacit agreement is reciprocal. In Italy things are done differently. He who arrives first never goes away. He knows it is annoying, but he pleases himself. As he came out of the dressing-room the Venetian came across Madame Casacci in the wings, and he spoke with her, complimenting her on the applause which she had drawn from the monarch, and joking and making a few light-hearted witticisms. But suddenly the Podstoli reappeared: he must have come out of the dressing-room where the Venetian had left him, for no other purpose than to follow him and attack him. He planted himself in front of him, and looking at him uncivilly from head to foot, as tailors do, he asked what he was doing there with that lady. The Venetian, who had never spoken to that gentleman before, was not a little surprised, and answered that he was there to pay his respects. The Podstoli then asked him if he loved her, and he replied that he did. His interrogator added that he too loved her, and that it was not his habit to suffer rivals. The Venetian replied that he had not been informed of this whim of his. 'Well then,' said the Podstoli, 'you must yield her to me.' The Venetian, in a somewhat joking tone, said: 'Very well, sir. To a fine knight like you, there is no one who should not yield. I therefore yield this delightful lady to you completely, with all the rights which I can possibly have over her.' 'Very good,' added the Podstoli, with a sour face. 'But a coward that yields, when he has yielded *f...t le camp*.' These words, which I have written in French because we were speaking in French, and because they are hard to translate, are the most vile which can be used to mean *go away* by a man who is haughty, superior, and uncivil towards a very base man,

14

to whom he speaks in this way not only to indicate his deepest scorn but also to threaten sudden violence if he is not immediately obeyed.

The Venetian, who unfortunately – or perhaps fortunately – understood French, and who from his earliest years had been accustomed to resist those first impulses which, truly unworthy of a rational man, can transform him into a beast – and because of which the laws have laughably insisted that we should show mercy – was able to control himself, and resist the strong temptation to kill the brute on the spot. He set off towards the steps which led down from the theatre, only saying to his proud insulter, before taking one step to go away, and looking steadily into his face, and placing his left hand on the hilt of his sword: '*C'en est trop.*' ['This is too much.'] There was no doubt that this was a challenge, because it might have been even more laconic: his hand on the hilt of his sword would have sufficed, or a movement, a gesture, a flicker of the eye. While the Venetian was going away very slowly, the Podstoli said in a loud voice, so that it could be heard by two officers who were not very far away: 'That Venetian coward has made the right decision in going away: *j'allois l'envoier se faire f...e.*' ['I was going to send him off to f*** himself.'] To these words the other, without turning round, replied: '*Un poltron venitien enverrà dans un moment à l'autre monde un brave polonois.*' ['A Venetian coward will shortly send a brave Pole to the next world.'] If to the word 'coward', which was rude enough in itself, that man had not added the word 'Venetian', the other might have borne the affront. But there is, I believe, no man who can stomach a word which vilifies his nation. Having said this, the Venetian, although the night was very dark, went to the door of the theatre to wait for him with the intention of coming to blows in some place or other, to give

15

or receive some sword-thrusts, and so bring the affair to a conclusion. But he waited in vain for half an hour without seeing anyone, and an icy rain was falling onto the snow. So, half-frozen, he decided to have his carriage fetched and to go to the home of the Prince Palatine of Russia, where he knew that the King was to dine.

The Venetian showed his wisdom in suffering the insolent offence of the Podstoli in the place where he was: since the King was nearby with his guards, every violent motion of his, however slight, would have been a matter of great consequence. But he could not conceal the affair, since two officers had been on the scene, and also Biszewski, who was the faithful friend of the Podstoli. He was therefore seriously perplexed.

Without his having decided anything, the horses brought him at a rapid trot to the Prince Palatine's house, where he found the flower of their nobility assembled. As soon as he saw him, the Prince set up a game of tressette[5] and, as he usually did, took him for his partner. But he, as he played, did nothing but make mistakes. When the Prince reproached him for this, he replied that his mind was miles away. The Prince, saying quietly that one could not have one's mind elsewhere when playing cards, threw the cards on the table and the game ended. Then an official arrived from the Court to say that the King would not be coming to dinner, so the Palatine ordered the tables to be set immediately.

The poor injured stranger was very sorry that the King was not coming, since he would have told His Majesty of the injury which the Podstoli had done him, and the sovereign would have settled it all, obliging the unjust offender to make adequate compensation to the man he had offended; but the matter had to be settled in a very different way.

They all sat down to dinner, and he sat at the head of the oblong table with the Prince Palatine on his left. The talk was of pleasant things, and it was far from his mind to talk about his misfortune, which he would have preferred to remain hidden from everyone. However, in the middle of the meal Prince Kaspr Lubomirski, a general in the service of Russia, arrived and went to sit at the opposite end of the table, at which there must have been about thirty people dining. When this Prince came face to face with him at the other end of the table, he said to him in a loud voice that he was sorry about the unfortunate incident in which he had been involved at the theatre. To these good wishes, which cut him to the quick, and which he had been sincerely hoping not to receive from anyone, because the affair was not yet public, he did not have the heart to reply. Nevertheless, Prince Kaspr continued to console him, perhaps maliciously, telling him that the offender was drunk, that it was best to forget the matter, that the esteem which everyone had for him would not be diminished because of it, together with a hundred similar cruel words of comfort, which far from calming him, stirred him up. The Palatine, noticing this, asked him in a kindly way and in a low voice what the matter was. He begged His Highness to wait until after the meal when he would tell him in private. He could however see at the other end of the table everyone talking and listening to Prince Kaspr, and the Venetian was covered in shame to find all eyes fixed in that direction.

When the dinner was over, the Prince Palatine drew him aside, and had from him all the wretched story in faithful detail. As he listened to him, that Prince had grief written all over his majestic countenance, and he blushed that in Warsaw an honest man should be subjected to such vile affronts. When he had finished his account he asked the Prince what he would advise him to do in the situation in which he found himself. To this request the Prince replied that it was not his habit ever to advise anyone in a case like this. 'The honest man in a predicament like this,' he said with a sigh, 'should do much or nothing at all.' So saying, the Prince withdrew, and the other, having had his pelisse brought to him, left the palace, stepped into his coach, and went off home, where he lay down immediately and slept soundly for six hours. When he awakened, he took some medicine which he been taking for two weeks, in order to cure himself of a certain illness which was afflicting him at that time, and which obliged him after taking it to remain in bed for at least six hours. Having done that, he set about dispatching his letters, and particularly those which on that day – a Wednesday, the day on which the royal dispatches left for Italy – it was vital that he should send to the Court. As he began on this work he went over what had happened to him with the Podstoli on the evening of the night which had not yet passed; he reconsidered his own behaviour and pondered the words which the Prince Palatine of Russia had said to him when he had asked for his advice, and in those words which had denied him advice he found advice: 'Much or nothing.'

He thought first of 'nothing', and he remembered how Plato in his *Gorgias* said that heroism consists in not injuring anyone, whence it follows he is more to be praised who suffers an injury than the other who has managed to inflict it with impunity. Since he was not a soldier – a profession which obliges him who follows it to convince the world that he holds his life lightly, and to avoid the reputation of cowardice as he would avoid infamy – he was dispensed from the sovereign requirement of killing the man who had insulted him, or having himself killed by that man. For this reason he could boldly and proudly declare himself a follower of the great philosopher who clearly states 'that it is less dishonourable to put up with grave injuries than to inflict them.' Then he considered also that this was a Christian's maxim, and he rebuked himself because Plato had come to his mind an instant before the Gospel. But then, as he reflected further, with that cursed pride which is so much a part of human nature, he considered the way of thinking of the philosophers of the Court, who expressly or tacitly insist that honour should reign, and that this honour should be modelled on the military code, to expedite whose triumph monarchs themselves ostentatiously wear military insignia. He saw that if he were to act in the Platonic way, he would be a good Christian and a fine philosopher, but no less dishonoured and despised on that account, and perhaps driven from the Court and excluded from noble assemblies with great opprobrium.

This is the way things are these days. It is the duty of philosophy to lament it, while those who would like to follow philosophy's maxims ought to live anywhere but at Court.

If the unfortunate injured party had taken the decision to swallow the bitter pill peacefully and in silence (or to reveal the affair only to that neutral band of idlers who display the cold and empty title of common friends), he would have found crowds of mediators who, with the appearance of the greatest zeal, would have worked hard for a reconciliation, all of them axiomatically more in favour of the offender than of the one who was offended. Such is the malignity of human nature that people always enjoy the harm that has been done, and are therefore always drawn towards the one who has done it, secretly laughing at him who has suffered the outrage, and endeavouring to minimise it with sophistical reasons under the specious pretext of a praiseworthy desire for peace.

The true friend of a man who has been insulted either helps him to get revenge, or he does as did the Prince Palatine of Russia – he deplores it, and leaves it to him to do what is suggested by his own idea of honour, whose quality no one can guess. In general the mediator knows what the offended party desires. 'A man who acts in this way is a friend only in name, a name which he does not deserve, when he claims that his friend wants what he does not want, but what in his opinion his friend should want, and who is not content to give advice but, getting above himself, affects a superiority in aims and wisdom.' These words are Cicero's, and that is why I have set them here.

The injured Venetian, having considered all this in less time than I have taken to write it, decided to do *much*. He resolved to challenge that insulting knight to a duel, the only means in that land, and in others too, by which a man who has been injured by someone who possesses no rights over him, can wash away the stain left by the injury he has received.

If the injured parties, by bringing the offenders to justice, could delude themselves into thinking that they would obtain from the judge a heavy sentence in their favour, it might be that duels would not occur so frequently, despite the unfortunate maxim of 'the point of honour'. But experience shows that they cannot hope for anything more than a cold excuse or a ridiculous retraction, which according to certain thinkers seems more apt to spread the stain than to wash it away. In England, however, a man who has said an offensive word to another, if he cannot prove in Court that he has said the truth, is more or less ruined.

Such are the thoughts which lead some men to challenge those who have insulted them, and often even get themselves killed.

The modern philosopher Rousseau has a saying which is pertinent here. He says that those who are truly avenged are not those who kill, but those who compel their offenders to kill them. I confess I am not so high-minded as to be of the same opinion as the sublime Genevan in this, even though the thought is strange and new, and readily admits, for anyone who wishes justify it, subtle and heroic reasonings, of the kind hunted for by modern thinkers, who consider themselves truly blessed when they can by sophistry make paradoxes into aphorisms. 'The Podstoli will either,' reasoned the Venetian, 'accept my challenge or refuse it. If he accepts it, then I shall have satisfaction, whatever the outcome of the duel: if he refuses, I shall nevertheless be avenged, because by challenging him I show that I do not fear him, and that there is an intrepid heart in my breast and a mind that leads me not to consider my own life once it is overshadowed by an insult. By taking such a step I compel him to respect me, and to repent of having offended a man whom he can no longer proclaim to be a coward, since he sees him ready to sacrifice himself to his own honour.' One might add that if the Podstoli refused the duel, the Venetian would have the upper hand and be able to accuse him of cowardice and to say openly that he no longer considered himself stained by that injury, since he had discovered that the offender was a base coward, by whom a man of honour can never be offended, since he is regarded with contempt as a madman.

Challenging someone who has been offensive to a duel is the natural impulse of anyone who has been brought up to be moderate and check his first brutal reactions. A barbaric man, who, because of his noble upbringing, has not been accustomed to restrain his first impulses, repels an offence with an offence and tries, spurred on by his passions and his natural desire for revenge, to take the life of the man who has insulted him, without exposing himself to the risk of becoming a victim of his own sense of what is right.

As a result of this reasoning, based on a knowledge of the human heart and the strength of prevailing prejudices, he prepared without any loss of time to send the knight a note which did in fact challenge him, but whose tone was such that it could not be condemned by the law in any circumstances which might occur, in a land where duels were forbidden under penalty of death. Here are the contents of the note, a faithful copy of which is in the hands of him who is now writing this account:

Monseigneur,

Hyer au soir sur le théâtre Votre Excellence m'a insulté de gaieté de coeur, et elle n'avoit ni raison ni droit d'en agir ainsi vis-à-vis de moi. Cela étant, je juge, Monseigneur, que vous me haissez; et que par consequent vous voudriez me faire sortir du nombre des vivans. Je puis, et je veux contenter Votre Excellence.

Aiéz la complaisance, Monseigneur, de me prendre dans votre équipage, et de me conduire où ma défaite ne puisse pas vous rendre fautif vis-à-vis des lois de la Pologne, et où je puisse jouir du même avantage, si Dieu m'assiste au point de tuer Votre Excellence.

Je ne vous ferois pas, Monseigneur, cette proposition sans l'idée que j'ai de votre generosité.

J'ai l'honneur d'être, Monseigneur, de Votre Excellence le très humble, et très obeissant serviteur

G.C.

ce mecredy 5 Mars 1766, à la pointe du jour.

[*Your Excellency,*

At the theatre yesterday evening you offended me without cause and without having any right to act towards me in such a way. That being the case, I judge, Your Excellency, that you hate me and consequently desire to remove me from the land of the living. I am able and willing to satisfy you.

May it please Your Excellency to take me with you in your carriage, and to conduct me to a place where my death may not cause you to violate the laws of Poland, and where I may enjoy the same advantage, if with God's help I succeed in killing you.

I should not make this proposal to you, Your Excellency, if I did not know how magnanimous you are.

I have the honour to be Your Excellency's very humble and obedient servant

G. C.

Today, Wednesday, 5 March 1766, at daybreak.]

Having copied and sealed this letter, he shook awake a Cossack who always slept fully clothed across the threshold of his room, and told him to take the note to the Court to the apartment of the Podstoli, and ordered him to hand it over without saying who sent it and to come back home immediately. This he did. Before half an hour had passed a page came from the Podstoli to deliver to the Venetian personally the following reply written in the Podstoli's hand and sealed with his arms.

Monsieur,

J'accepte votre proposition, mais vous aurez la bonté, Monsieur, de vouloir bien m'avertir quand j'aurai l'honneur de vous voir. Je suis très parfaitement, Monsieur,

Votre très humble , et très obeissant

Serviteur Branicki P.

5 Mars 1766

[*Sir,*

I accept your proposal, but beg you to have the goodness, sir, to inform me when I shall have the honour of seeing you.

I am truly, sir, your most humble and most obedient servant

Branicki P.]

From the noble brevity of this note one can see that the Podstoli did not hesitate one minute before accepting the challenge, and indeed that it was a pleasure to him to receive it. Recognising in an instant that he had offended a man who did not fear him, there came to him a thought which pierced his heart: he was afraid that the challenger might imagine that he had to do with a coward and was perhaps terrifying him. He reflected that the man who had challenged him perhaps believed himself a better man than he was, and was laughing at him. Then it came into his mind that he had perhaps been unlucky enough to insult a brave man, and so he saw it as his religious duty to give him satisfaction, even by killing him if necessary, but at the same time honouring him who had wished to get himself killed rather than suffer the slightest injury from him. These reflections did not make him indifferent to the pleasure of another triumph. Therefore he hastened to accept the challenge, so that the other, supposing he were afraid, should not have time to get his courage up. There occurred to him also another malicious thought. He thought it possible that the challenger had hoped that he would not accept the challenge. So he accepted, and he deluded himself that he had stumbled upon some pusillanimity which might then justify him, demonstrating to the whole world that after all he had only insulted a coward. However, he did hope deep down in his heart that the challenger was a man of valour, since it never happens that a man of worth thinks another better than he is, and therefore he foresaw a more glorious victory for himself, and in his heart he was certain he would be victorious. These are the thoughts which on occasions like this dwell in the mind of the man who is truly noble. The noble man who has offended someone never goes hunting for subterfuges which might exempt him from giving the offended party complete satisfaction. Those who are not ready to give satisfaction are worthless people, even if they demonstrate that the people they offended deserved to be offended, or that they are cowardly souls insensible to any affront, or rather that they are compelled by the lowliness of their condition or their dutiful subordination to pretend to be so.

The Venetian, glad to have brought the matter to a crux, replied immediately thus:

Je me rendrai, Monseigneur, demain matin jeudi à l'antichambre de V.E.; j'attendrai votre réveil, et j'aurai toute la journée libre. Vous ne sauriez penser, Monseigneur, combien je me croie honnoré par la reponse que V.E. m'a faite. J'ai l'honneur etc.

[*Tomorrow morning, Thursday, I shall wait in your ante-chamber until Your Excellency awakes, and I shall be free for the whole day. Your Excellency cannot conceive how honoured I feel myself to be by your response. I have the honour of being etc.*]

He consigned this reply to the same page, who returned a quarter of an hour later with this note from the impatient Podstoli.

Je ne consens pas a transporter à demain une affaire qu'on doit terminer aujourd'hui. Je vous attens chez moi d'abord. Marquez moi en attendant les armes, et le lieu etc.

[*I do not agree to putting off till tomorrow an affair which ought to be settled today. I expect you here immediately. Meanwhile, name the arms and the place etc.*]

The Venetian replied to him:

Je n'aurai point d'autre arme que mon epée, et quant au lieu ce sera celui où V.E. me conduira hors de la starostie de Varsovie; mais pas avant demain, puisqu'aujourd'hui j'ai un paquet à remettre au roi; j'ai pris médecine, et j'ai un testament à faire. Je suis etc.

[*I shall have no other arms but my sword, and, as to the place, I shall be pleased wherever Your Excellency conducts me outside the jurisdiction of Warsaw; but I repeat that it will have to be tomorrow, because today I have a packet to send to the King, I have taken some medicine, and I must make my will. I am etc.*]

Half an hour after this letter had been sent, the Venetian, who was in bed, was rather surprised to see the Podstoli appear in his room alone, and to hear him say that he had to speak to him about a confidential matter. Once they heard these words, some subordinates who happened to be in the room did not wait to be asked to leave. The two principal actors remained alone, and the Podstoli sat down on the bed. I hope the reader will pardon it, but he who is writing this feels the need to become dramatic in order to be faithful and clear in his account.

PODSTOLI [*sitting on the Venetian's bed*]: I have come to ask you if you are making fun of me.

VENETIAN: How could you think it! I have the greatest respect, sir, for your person that anyone could have.

PODSTOLI: You send me a challenge, and when I accept it immediately, you try to play for time. This is not fair. If you really feel the affront which you insist I have subjected you to, then you should be in more of a hurry than I am to unburden yourself of it.

VENETIAN: I feel that that unwelcome load is already considerably lightened by the fact that you are engaged to fight with me. A delay of twenty-four hours is not very great: our quarrel, now that we have reached an agreement, has become such that it may be conducted courteously. Who says that we have to rush into a fight today rather than tomorrow?

PODSTOLI: My conviction is that if we do not fight immediately we shall not fight at all.

VENETIAN: What can stop us?

PODSTOLI: Both being arrested by order of the King.

VENETIAN: But how? Who will inform the King of our intention?

PODSTOLI: I certainly will not.

VENETIAN: And neither will I.

PODSTOLI: I do not know that. I am aware of the tricks your nation gets up to.

VENETIAN: I understand; but you are completely mistaken. My nation has taught skill and civil politeness to yours, and for my part I shall compel you to respect it. Know then that I am so far from thinking up tricks to avoid measuring swords with you that, in order to have such an honour, I would travel a hundred leagues on foot, so great is the esteem in which I hold your person. And know also that I have one advantage over you: I do not think you capable of any cowardly action.

PODSTOLI: I am glad that you know me so well. I am not obliged to have the good opinion of you which you have of me, because – as you must be aware – I do not know you. I must say to you, however, that your challenge makes me have high hopes of you, although your postponement of the test shows you to me in a very unfavourable light. Let's stop talking: let's fight today, and then you can give convincing proof that you do not have in mind those designs which I have been led to suspect you are hatching.

VENETIAN: I have taken some medicine, I have some very important letters to write, and I must draw up a small will.

PODSTOLI: Six hours from now the medicine will have worked; you can write the letters after we have fought, and if you lose your life, believe me that those who remain in the world after you are gone will not regard the lack of those letters as a serious matter; as for the will, you really make me laugh: you are taking the duel too seriously; you should know that one does not die quite so easily. Do not be afraid. I should like you to think of this matter as I do: a duel is a mere bagatelle. In conclusion I say to you simply that, since you have challenged me and I have accepted, I have the right to tell you that I wish to fight today, or not at all. You understand.

VENETIAN: I understand you so well that you have persuaded me, in fact convinced me. I shall be ready to go with you to fight today, three hours after midday.

PODSTOLI: That pleases me. Bravo! But I have one more thing to say to you.

VENETIAN: Please say it.

PODSTOLI: You wrote to me that your chosen arm would be your sword; but that is simply not possible.

VENETIAN: Why?

PODSTOLI: I can be excused from fighting with the sword against any man whom I do not know, because you might well be such a skilful master of that art that you could have too great an advantage over me: I have no more skill in it than is obligatory for any knight whose profession is war.

VENETIAN: You could refuse a fencing-master, I grant you, but not me whom I honestly believe to have less skill in it than you, since your profession was never mine.

PODSTOLI: I repeat that I do not know you. We shall fight with pistols. Those arms are equal, and with them the bravery can readily be equal.

VENETIAN: Pistols are too dangerous. It could happen that to my great grief I had the misfortune to kill you, and equally you might, against your will, perhaps without hating me very much, kill me. Therefore no pistols. With a sword in my hand I hope that I shall not chance to wound you mortally, and a few drops of your blood would be ample compensation to me for the affront with which you have sullied me. Similarly, I shall do my best to protect myself, so that you will only manage to prick me lightly, and that small amount of my blood will suffice to cleanse me from the ugly stain with which you have blackened me. In conclusion, remember that you have given me the choice of weapons. I have chosen the sword, and I wish to fight only with the sword, and I have the right to maintain that it is no longer your place to refuse it.

PODSTOLI: That is true. I cannot deny it. I have no right to retract my word. But if I were to ask it of you, as one asks a favour of a friend?

VENETIAN: A favour! You barbarian, you!

PODSTOLI: Yes, a favour. Just listen to me. We shall begin our duel with one good pistol-shot each, and then, if you wish, we shall fight with swords until we are tired of it. This is the favour which I beg of you. Can you deny me such a slight favour?

VENETIAN: Well, if it is true, as you assure me, that this is a favour you are asking, then to please you in this matter becomes a pleasure to me also. I shall perform this service for you, and we shall take a good shot at each other with pistols. But I have to laugh, because it is not a thing we shall enjoy very much. I beg you meanwhile to bring two duelling pistols with you, since I only have dress-pistols.

PODSTOLI: I shall bring excellent arms. You have obliged me considerably. I thank you, and I respect you. Give me your hand. You will come with me, and we shall go and fight each other with the most complete reciprocal satisfaction, and then we shall be good friends. I shall come to fetch you three hours after midday precisely. You promise me you will be ready?

VENETIAN: I promise you, sir, that you will not even need to climb this long flight of steps. You will find me very prompt.

PODSTOLI: That is all I desire. Goodbye.

As soon as the Venetian was alone, he placed in a packet under a seal the most important writings which he had with him.

Then, having considered carefully who would be most helpful to him, whom he could trust the most, he decided on a Venetian dancing-master who was then living in Warsaw, called Vincenzo Campioni. He sent someone to find this man and, giving the packet to him, asked him if he was ready to swear to execute faithfully a commission which was more important to him than life. He swore. So the Venetian said to him: 'If at the end of this day you are able to speak to me, you will return this packet to me: and if you are not, you will go and give it into His Majesty's own hands. If this commission of mine leads you at this moment to form some suspicions, I warn you that if you dare to communicate them to anyone you will be a traitor to me, and my most atrocious enemy.'

This man, who knew what had occurred between the Venetian and the Grand Butler the day before, and had by chance seen the latter that same morning leaving the Venetian's house, guessed there was a duel in the offing. He was very fearful for the life of the Venetian, whom he had reason to be fond of, and he had the option of going immediately to inform the sovereign of everything, in which case the conflict would not have taken place and he would have removed his friend from all danger of losing his life or his liberty. But he did not do so. If he had done so, he would have been a wretch, a perjurer, a coward, a traitor, in short a false friend.

A true friend will do nothing except what is to the complete satisfaction of his friend; he considers all that ill done which to someone else might seem better done because done in a different way. The true friend deals admirably with those matters where interest or glory forbids a complete expla-nation. It is easy to make him see and understand what one does not wish to show him or say to him, and he is not offended by this reserve, and he does not act with any less zeal than he would if the friend had explained everything to him and trusted to his discretion. In short the true friend cannot be happy with himself unless he gives satisfaction to the person for whom he is working, having no other interest in what he does apart from his friend's.

The false friend, on the contrary, is always dissatisfied with the way in which he is employed; he abounds in silent reflections; he always finds some personal interest in the matter which is entrusted to him; and he always has some secret purpose which he would not dare to confess. When it is essential to get to the heart of the matter, he carries it out *ad verbum*[6], and when it is essential not to deviate in any way from the letter, he devises whimsical refinements. He has always read wrongly or understood wrongly, and with him no one has ever explained himself clearly enough.

Once the Venetian had the package in safe hands, he thought of enjoying a choice dinner. Therefore he gave the requisite orders for it, and sent a message to ask two learned young knights, affectionate brothers who honoured him with their friendship, to come and dine with him at midday. Excellent food, good wine, and the good company of friends who are well chosen and above all well-disposed, compose a nourishment which raises a healthy man to the highest degree of perfection of which he is capable. Such a meal puts all the fluids in a steady balance, invigorates the solid parts, gives all necessary vigour to every physical faculty, and adds a joyfulness to the spirits which rouses all the powers that combine with his kindled courage to make that individual most apt to undertake any important action in which he has need of his entire self, and in which above all he must not be to blame if he fails, enabling those who examine his actions after the event to say that he acted badly. All this was understood by the Venetian. He knew that the faculties of mind and body are left weakened and dormant in those who eat and drink excessively, and that for those people, the taking of nourishment is followed by that lethargy called sleep, which their nature would not promptly require if they had not wearied, oppressed, and deadened it with superfluous, gross, or badly prepared food. The French cuisine, which justly enjoys universal applause, does not generate in those who know its value either untimely sleep or indigestion; nor does it make him regretful who is able to enjoy its delights without giving way to greed. There is no man or woman who, after a choice meal, is not more attractive, more eloquent, more animated, more courteous, more judicious, and more self-possessed, full of fine thoughts and unusual ideas which are capable of providing honourable and legitimate pleasures to this wretched human race, which, left to itself, is an inexhaustible fount of unhappiness, boredom, and troublesome disagreements.

And so, just as bodily health comes from good food, there is no doubt that spiritual peace derives from it also, since that cannot have any other impulse than those it receives from physical impressions. So woe betide those who have earned a name for being great eaters. Among these, very few know what it is to eat well; greed is their god, and when we look at them we do not see, either in their bodies or in their spirits, any sign of that happy nourishment which I have praised above. Eating too much makes people ill; it shortens their lives, and it dulls the soul's faculties.

Dulcia se in bilem vertent, stomacoque tumultum
Lenta feret pituita. Vides ut pallidus omnis

Cena desurgat dubia? quin corpus onustum
Hesternis vitiis animum quoque pregravat una,
Atque affigit humo divinae particulam aurae.[7]

When he had dined, and mixed some pure Burgundy wine with the food, he asked the company to leave him. On days when there is a postal service this request is not regarded as impolite. Once he was alone, he arranged things so that he would not have to keep the Podstoli waiting, since according to their agreement he was shortly due to arrive. He arrived at the appointed time at a fast trot, with six horses drawing his English carriage which could hold four passengers. The Venetian immediately went down the steps, and he was at the door of the carriage when the Podstoli was just about to step from it. Besides him, there was in the carriage a chamberlain, a field adjutant-general of the King, and one of his chasseurs. The adjutant-general, who was sitting by the Podstoli, gave up his place to the Venetian and sat in the front. But the Venetian, still standing on the footboard, paused before entering when he saw at a glance that there was – besides the postilions, chasseurs, outriders, grooms, and pages – also another adjutant-general on horseback with a servant leading two harnessed horses. Then he turned his head and said to two of his servants, who were about to mount behind the carriage, that they should not follow him but should stay there to await his orders. The Grand Butler, when he heard that, said to him: 'Let them follow you, because you might happen to have need of them.' The Venetian replied: 'Since I cannot bring with me servants who are equal to yours in number, I don't want even this wretched pair. You have enough to look after me if I am in need. May I hope for that?' 'Yes,' he answered, 'and I promise you on my honour as a knight that they will look after you in preference to myself.' And as he said that, he stretched out his hand which the other shook as he entered the coach and sat down by him. They left immediately, and he neither knew where they were going nor cared to ask.

They were still inside the city when it occurred to the Venetian that it would be a politeness to break their silence. And so he asked the Podstoli if he was thinking of making his home in Warsaw in the coming summer. To this question he replied: 'That is what I had planned to do, but you may be the reason why I have to do otherwise.' The Venetian replied that he hoped he would not be the cause of anything to displease him. 'I am already coming to think,' continued the other, 'that you have the character of a gentleman, or that you have served in war...' The Venetian interrupted him to say that he had never felt so noble as he did on that day. '...But why,' he continued, looking the Podstoli straight in the face, 'do you ask me this?' 'I don't know why,' replied the other, lightly and with a smile, 'except that I don't know what else to say. Let's not speak of it any more, I beg you.' And they did not speak of it any more. Despite the thick snow, the horses ran very well, and two and a half hours before nightfall they came to Wola, a large garden owned by Count von Brühl, a great general of the royal artillery who was at that time in Dresden.

Going into the garden, the Podstoli, with the Venetian at his side and his whole company following him, stopped under an oval-shaped pergola not more than ten poles long, with a stone table in the middle of it. On this table his chasseur, to whom he had made a sign, placed a pair of long pistols of shining polished steel, and with them a small bag of metal implements, and a container from which he took powder, balls, and a pair of scales, with a sort of little mill which was needed to load the

35

arms. After he had demonstrated to the two principal actors, who stood looking at him attentively while he worked, that the pistols were empty, he chose two suitable balls equal in weight and calibre, and weighed out two equal quantities of powder, with which he loaded the pistols. Once they were loaded, the Grand Butler courteously asked the Venetian to take up whichever pistol he preferred, saying that he would use the other. The Venetian was prevented from making his choice promptly by the voice of the King's adjutant-general. 'This,' he said in German, 'is a duel, something which I cannot allow.' 'You do not have to know,' replied Branicki, 'what it is. Be silent, and wait and see, and when you have seen then you can speak.' 'I cannot be ignorant of anything,' repeated the other. 'We are in the jurisdiction of Warsaw, I am on guard duty today, you have tricked me into leaving the Court to make me an accomplice to a crime which will bring down His Majesty's anger upon me. Since you have made me come here, I oppose your intention.' 'Why do want to oppose it?' said the other, smiling. 'The King will pardon you, when he knows that you were surprised into being present at the action, and for the rest you need not worry, since I willingly take upon myself all the consequences of the affair, at which for good reasons I wish you to be present. Do you understand? So move two paces away and let us get on with it. I am an honourable knight, and I must give satisfaction to whoever believes he has the right to ask it of me. I wish to show this Italian *que je sais pajer de ma personne* [that I can answer for it myself], which has always been enough for me.' 'It is then up to you, Signor C***' insisted the adjutant-general to the Venetian, 'to avoid this duel. I invite you to submit any grievance of yours to His Majesty, and I warn you that you cannot fight here, since you are in the royal jurisdiction.' The

Venetian then replied that he was not thinking of fighting, but of defending himself, something which he would do even if he were in church; but that if it was a question of giving some sign of his veneration for the King (and as he said that, he raised his hat) by submitting himself to him for compensation for the wrong which the Podstoli had done, he was ready to make that submission, provided he was asked to do so by the Podstoli himself. He was indeed ready to require no further satisfaction if the Podstoli was willing then, in his presence, to say to him 'that he was sorry that yesterday he had said those outrageous words.' At this the Podstoli, with a sour expression, looked the Venetian straight in the face and said to him: '*Monsieur! Je ne suis pas venu ici pour raisonner, mais pour me battre.*' ['I have not come here to talk, but to fight.'] Then the adjutant-general raised his eyes to heaven, struck his forehead with his right hand, and retired two paces. The Podstoli calmly discarded his pelisse, which a page took care of, and unfastened his sword which he gave to the same page. The other would have been ashamed not to copy him: so he did so, and gave his sword to the same page, but regretfully, since he did not know how the affair would go, and by doing so he left himself unarmed. For a moment he thought that he could keep his sword at his side, and remind the Podstoli of their agreement to draw their swords after one pistol-shot, but he was afraid of showing himself to be less courteous than the knight and motivated too much by ill-will. Then the Podstoli asked him again to take one of the pistols that were laid crosswise on the table. This he did, taking that one whose butt was turned towards him, and the Podstoli grasped the other, saying to him these exact words: '*L'arme que vous tenez, Monsieur, est parfaite; j'en suis garant.*' ['That weapon which you have chosen is perfect; I myself guarantee it.'] To this formal act of politeness it occurred to the other to make this only too true reply: '*Actuellement, Monseigneur, je le crois, mais je ne le saurai qu'après en avoir faite l'experience contre votre tête; prenez garde à vous.*' ['At this moment, sir, I believe that; but I shall not know it until I have tried it out against your head; so stay on guard.'] They said no more but, with their weapons lowered and looking each other in the face, they slowly moved ten paces back, so that they were exactly fifty feet apart, a distance which was almost the length of the pergola.

The Venetian, who had already raised his pistol, holding its muzzle downwards, turned sideways, as if they were about to fight with swords, but without stretching out his arm, and in this position, raising his hat and then bringing it down to his left knee, he said to the Podstoli: '*Votre Excellence m'honnorera de tirer le premier.*' ['Your Excellency will do me the honour of firing first.'] He replied: '*Mettez-vous en garde.*' ['On guard!'] The other immediately put on his hat, brought his left hand down to his left side, raised the other hand which held the pistol, and when he saw it was aimed at the Podstoli's body, fired it. At the same instant the knight fired his pistol, so that those who were nearby heard only one shot; so it is true that they fired at the same time. If the Podstoli had not wasted time it is certain that he would have fired before the other, and would perhaps have killed him; but he wasted at least three seconds in replying: '*Mettez-vous en garde*' (something which it was not up to him to think about) and drawing himself up, and stretching his arm out as far as he could, so that the other could no longer see his head. He supposed that the Venetian was aiming at his head, because of what he had said to him, which he only said as a manner of speaking, because the duellist who aims at his adversary's head, and not his breast, puts himself at a great disadvantage. The Venetian, after he had said to his adversary: 'Do me the honour of firing first,' did not think himself obliged to suppose that the other would delay, or obliged to prolong the civilities by waiting for the other's convenience. He did not think either of the slight advantage of making himself a smaller target by drawing himself up, but in the not inconvenient position in which he was, without moving at all, or batting an eyelid, with his pulse steady, he fired. And in the same instant he felt himself wounded in his left hand, which he immediately concealed in the pocket of his jacket, and he saw the Podstoli preventing himself from falling with his left hand on the ground, and he heard him say: '*Je suis blessé.*' ['I am wounded.'] The Venetian threw his pistol away and ran to him, but halfway there he saw two Polish sabres raised above him, ready to cut him to pieces. And they would already have come down on him, because he had stopped and was standing stock-still awaiting their downward strokes, if the soldier, who was hardly able to hold himself up, had not cried in a furious voice when he saw those wicked men: '*Canaille, respectez ce cavalier.*' ['Scoundrels, respect this knight.']⁸ At these words those rogues (true friends, however, to Branicki in their Polish way) were ashamed and they drew back. The Venetian ran to the left of the magnanimous man, and with his right hand under his arm lifted him, while on his other side the troubled general had run to his aid. In this way the Podstoli, bent double and supported by the two of them, and followed by his servants, came to the inn which was a hundred paces away. There, stretched out on a large chair, he wished to see his wound. He stayed on his back, and he was quickly unbuttoned and, when the servants raised his shirt above his breast, it could be seen that the ball had entered his body between the third and fourth false ribs on his right side, and had exited diagonally for the distance of a span towards the centre of the left upper side of his abdomen, leaving his intestines unscathed, so extended and stretched out had he been when he received the shot. While his servants were washing from his stomach the blood which was all over him, the Venetian, who stood by his side, noticed that from time to time the Podstoli turned his gaze on his stomach too. Then, casting a glance at himself, he noticed that he too was streaming with blood issuing from his stomach. He marvelled at this, but made no movement.

When the Podstoli saw his own terrible wound, he kept a calm countenance, and ordered all his servants to race to the city in search of a surgeon, and to the other, who was supporting himself on the arm of the chair, he said: '*Monsieur, vous m'avez tué; j'ai le cordon de l'Aigle Blanc, et une charge dans la couronne; les duels sont défendus,... nous sommes dans le district de Varsovie; vous serez condamné à mort; sauvez vous; servez vous de mes chevauz, dont je croiòis de devoir me servir moi même, allez en Livonie, et si vous n'avez pas d'argente, acceptez ma bourse.*' ['You have killed me; I have the Order of the White Eagle, and a position under the Crown; duelling is prohibited, and we are in the jurisdiction of Warsaw; you will be condemned to death; flee: make use of my horses, which I thought I would have to use myself; take refuge in Livonia; and if you have no money, accept my purse.'] The Venetian, in admiration of such virtue, answered him with anguish in his soul: '*J'accepterois vos offres, Monseigneur, si je pensois a me sauver. Je vais à Varsovie me faire soigner de mes blessures, et je veux esperer que celle dont vous m'avez forcé à être l'auteur n'est pas dangereuse. Si je suis coupable de mort, je vais porter ma tête aux pieds du trone.*' ['I would accept your kind offers, sir, if I were thinking of flight. I am going to Warsaw to have my wounds treated, and I hope that the wound which you obliged me to give you is not dangerous. If I am guilty of murder, then I shall take my head to the foot of the throne.'] Having said this, he placed a kiss on the other's forehead, which was wet with perspiration, and departed alone, rushing across a snow-covered field to catch up with a sledge which he saw coming along drawn at a rapid trot by two horses on the main road.

Without that sledge, sent to him by Providence, he would have found himself in a sorry state, because it would have been difficult for him to reach the city on foot, difficult by reason of the amount of blood which he was losing from his hand and his stomach, and by reason of the extreme pain which the wound in his hand, as it worsened, was causing him.

In the circumstances he thought these following critical reflections were permissible.

He had been alone, while the Podstoli had been accompanied by ten people. And this was an outrage, because if the Podstoli had been killed, those friends of his would have killed his killer. That was made clear by what actually happened, and in matters of this kind honour and delicacy require that all possibilities should be taken into account. He had promised to fight with the sword after they had both fired their pistols, and by taking his sword off on the field of battle he constrained the other to do the same out of delicacy, so that he exposed him to very great danger. When the Venetian entered the coach, the Podstoli had sworn to him on his honour as a knight that he would cause him to be looked after in preference to himself, and he did not do so. Without that sledge, which was certainly sent to him by his guardian angel, he would have been exposed to the fury of the enraged Biszewski, who would have cut his head right off. (This devil arrived ten minutes later, as will be seen.)

The wound which the Podstoli had given him had struck him one inch below the navel: the ball had slid along the surface of his flesh – leaving him with only a slight wound, which nevertheless festered for many days, but which in fact he did not feel – and went into his left hand at the muscles of the thumb; it had stopped dead after shattering the first phalanx, and it had flattened, as was seen when the surgeon, in order to extricate it, had to cut open his hand at the other side above that spot.

Once he was on the sledge (by means of a sequin which he gave to the peasant who was driving it) he stretched out and covered himself with a mat, more for protection from the snow which was thrown up into the sledge by the horses' hooves, than for concealment. It was fortunate for him that he was covered up and therefore was not visible to anyone, since he had not gone a mile before he met with Biszewski. On horseback, with his sabre unsheathed, he was rushing along at full tilt in the hope of meeting him and cutting him into tiny pieces, as wholeheartedly as the loving shepherd fires his harquebus at the wolf which he meets dragging by the neck the ewe lamb which it has killed and stolen. Biszewski would have carried out this Polish plan without the slightest idea that a reasonable creature could have called his action less than honest, and even published it as an act of treachery: so heroic does an act of revenge seem to the Poles even today. He never imagined that the Venetian was under the mat, so he continued to race towards the inn where his wounded friend was waiting for treatment, and the Venetian arrived in Warsaw where, not finding anyone at the home of Prince Adam Czartoryski, he decided to take refuge in the Franciscan convent.

When he presented himself there, the porter, who did not know him, seeing him all smeared with blood and therefore supposing him to be a malefactor, was about to shut the door in his face; but the Venetian did not give him the chance: he entered by force, pushing him back and sending his legs up in the air. Then many of the brothers ran up, including the guardian himself who decided to let him have a room. In less than half an hour that room was full of the first lords of the Court, and the most accredited, since the Podstoli, although very brave and valiant, was considered essentially as the greatest enemy of the Polish nation, and since he was favoured by the King, he suffered from the curse which afflicts all favourites: he was feared and hated and envied by all. The most considerable of the great men therefore rushed to the convent, some to hear an account of the deed, some to assure the wounded man of their protection, some to offer him money, which he did not accept and which, if he had been wise, he would have accepted: but at that moment he found himself a prey to the demon of heroism. Necessity constrained him, however, to accept a hundred sequins from the Prince Palatine of Russia, and from his son Prince Adam the payment of his full board every day, not for him who was soon put on a diet, but for those who came at mealtimes to honour him. A French surgeon soon arrived to treat him. This surgeon first bled him, then cut open the upper part of his hand near the thumb, extracted the ball, stitched the wound with a silken thread, and prescribed a medicine for him. He said that the stomach of a wounded man should be completely emptied, and then left without any nourishment, apart from a simple broth. The Venetian did not dare to oppose this order, as he would have liked to when he heard that surgeon, who prided himself on understanding Latin, thunder out the aphorism *Vulnerati fame crucientur*[9]. The operation which the surgeon performed in order to extract the ball from his hand, was very painful, but he had learnt that there is no physical pain that a resolute mind cannot dissimulate: while the surgeon was operating, he gave an account of the event to the Palatine of Kalisz Twardowski and other great men who were standing by, and he managed, despite the pain he felt, not to show any sign of feeling it, and not to let his account be interrupted. '*I cannot*' is heard too often on the lips of mortals: it is very seldom on the lips of a man who really wishes to do something.

Prince Stanislas Lubomirski, at that time Strasnik, now Grand Marshal to the Crown, a learned and very pleasant gentleman, came to the Venetian's room at nightfall and told him of the more tragic event which had occurred after the duel. The furious Biszewski, when he arrived at Wola and saw his friend in that state, and knew that the Venetian had gone away, went into a frenzy. He remounted, determined to go and find him in his most secret hiding place, certainly not in order to challenge him to a duel, but to kill him personally wherever he found him. So he imagined that, when he returned to Warsaw, the Venetian had taken refuge in the home of Count Tomatis, who was also an Italian, and with whom he knew the Venetian was friendly. He may even have imagined that it was Tomatis himself who had urged the Venetian to call the Podstoli out, to avenge himself for a vile offence which he had had to suffer from the Podstoli a short while before, for which the Podstoli had deserved to be killed by Tomatis on the spot. But even if Biszewski had not thought that, he must certainly have believed that Tomatis was pleased by the way in which the Venetian had humiliated and punished the insolence of the overbold knight. It seemed to him, therefore, that Tomatis was unfit to live, and he went with the determination to kill him, if he did not find the other in his house.

He dismounted in the courtyard, climbed the steps in a rage, and, finding Tomatis in a good company of ladies and knights, demanded that he should immediately give the Venetian into his hands. When Tomatis replied that he did not know where that man was to be found, Biszewski drew a pistol from his pocket and fired it at the other's head. The shot went wide. Count Moscynski, Stolnik to the Crown, friendly, learned, generous, and full of life, who happened to be present, ran over to seize the enraged man and throw him out of the window. But unfortunately Biszewski, having his right hand free, slashed Moscynski twice, wounding his left arm and cutting his face with a long wound which ran down from the top of his left cheek to below his mouth on the right, cutting his lip, knocking out four of his teeth, and wounding his gums severely. Having done that, he rushed over to Prince Stanislas Lubomirski, who also happened to be one of the company, and holding a pistol to his breast, he took him by the arm and threatened him with death if he did not lead him safely to his horse which he had left in the courtyard. That man was a determined devil whose commands could not be ignored; the Prince conducted him to his horse in safety, and let him go to his ruin. Meanwhile, great was the uproar and fear in Warsaw. The word had got around that the Venetian had killed the Podstoli, and so the Ulans, with all those who were well-disposed towards him, rode throughout the streets looking for his killer, whom they would not have recognised, and slashing with their sabres anyone they came across who was not dressed like a Pole. All the merchants immediately closed their shops, as though afraid that an army of victorious Turks was about to enter the city and ransack it. It was fortunate that night was not long delayed.

The Venetian, the cause of all these incidents, was told of all this by the Prince who, with a pistol pointing at his breast, had helped the assassin to escape from the home of Count Tomatis unharmed. At that point a brother came into the room to say that the convent was completely surrounded by guards. The Prince said that this was by order of the Grand Marshal to the Crown, who had good reason to fear that the Ulans would come and force their way into the convent to seize the Venetian, and avenge the killing of their colonel with a massacre.

The Grand Marshal's tribunal, which is concerned with all criminal acts, and which condemns malefactors to death with no appeal, with the power to deny even the King's pardon, published against Biszewski, who had gone to take refuge in Königsberg, a strict sentence of banishment under penalty of death, with the confiscation of his goods and his degradation from the nobility.

At that instant there arrived an official from Prince Czartoryski, Palatine of Russia, who gave the Venetian a letter in which another one was enclosed. The one from the Prince said: '*Lisez, mon ami, ce que le roi m'écrit, et mettez votre esprit en repos.*' ['My friend, read what the King has written to me, and set your mind at rest.'] The enclosed letter was from the King, and it said: '*J'ai donné ordre, mon cher oncle, a mes chirurgiens d'avoir grand soin de Branicki, mais, j'ai su toute l'affaire, et je n'ai pas oublié le pauvre C*** Vous pouvez lui faire savoir que je lui fais grâce.*' ['My dear uncle, I have ordered my surgeons to take good care of Branicki, but I know all about the affair, and I have not forgotten poor C*** You may let him know that I pardon him.'] The Venetian kissed both the letters and, since he was in need of sleep, dismissed the company and went to bed.

On the following day the Podstoli sent one of his officers with his compliments, bringing him his sword and asking after his health, and letting him know that the wound he had received from him was not considered to be mortal, although it would take a long time to heal, since the integuments were considerably torn. The Venetian answered in kind, and these reciprocal visits continued every day.

Divine providence is apparent in everything that happens, and he is ungrateful who does not reflect on this and acknowledge it. The Podstoli did not perish in that duel because he had done what the Venetian had not done, and the Venetian would probably have fallen to the ground if he had done what the Podstoli certainly seemed to have done. As soon as Branicki had arranged with the other the time of their fight, and was certain of it, he went to confession and communion, and heard Mass with the most profound devotion. After that he remained alone for two hours, and he did not take food of any kind. The result showed that he owed his life to not having eaten: if he had eaten, the ball would have pierced him through his swollen intestines, and he would have died. On an empty stomach the Venetian would have spoken in a very different way, and would not have made such an impression on the other as to confuse him a little and so diminish that great ability of his which was known to all: whenever the Podstoli wished, he was able to hit the blade of a knife with a pistol-shot so that the ball was cut in two. The Venetian was not so well trained in shooting, and when he resolved to fight he put his trust in nothing but his knowledge that the ball, when fired, could not go otherwise than in a straight line. Consequently, having prevented any irregularity in his pulse with a good meal, he went to fight and gained the victory.

A certain person reasoned very thoughtlessly when he maintained that the Venetian would have performed a more than heroic action, and perhaps even made a very great fortune, if he had shot, not at the Podstoli's body, but into the air.

I believe that in this world when a shot is fired into the air, it comes about by chance, and is never premeditated. And if it were premeditated, I maintain that any man who went to fight with this idea in his mind, would be a madman, fit to be chained, since the first rule inculcated in anyone who is going to fight is to manage as soon as possible to render his enemy powerless to hurt him.

The art of driving an adversary to discharge his weapons in order to overcome him belongs to fighting with pistols on horseback, when one cannot fire without hitting the horse's rump, since the horse's head covers the rider, and killing the horse is a cowardly action. It is a different matter on foot. That is like fighting with swords: you take hold of the weapons, each looks to himself, but the courteous man does not fire unless he sees his adversary about to present his weapon, because presenting and firing happen simultaneously. The Venetian, pointing the muzzle of his pistol towards the ground, told the other to fire first, in order to confuse him, giving him in that critical moment a sign of respect which few men have the strength to think up; but replacing his hat, presenting, and firing were all done simultaneously. The other would certainly have fired first, if he had not lost time in drawing himself up and stretching out his arm, time which the Venetian would have been a fool to allow him.

Then, if the Podstoli had fired immediately and failed to hit, I, who know the Venetian, can assure the reader that he would immediately have run towards him, firing into the air, and clasping him in a friendly embrace, in one movement. These circumstances, which are all possible, show that firing into the air can never reasonably be the result of a premeditated plan.

But who knows if the Podstoli, having seen his shot wasted, would not have tried to recommence the duel! With certain proud people heroic actions are performed to their own harm. He is a wise man who avoids all occasion of such fights, but he who gets involved in them should think of nothing but getting rid of his enemy.

What remains to be considered is which of these two combatants gave, before fighting, evidence of being the more Christian. The Grand Butler went to confession; but I do not see how, if he made a full confession, he can have been absolved; and if he did not make a full confession, then I do not understand how he could be satisfied in his conscience with a falsely obtained absolution. I have been told that a soldier can easily find a confessor who will permit him to fight, and will *modo provisionis*[10] give him in anticipation absolution *in articulo mortis*[11]. This may well be, but the duel between these two was utterly beyond the sphere of those which religion at one time permitted, that is when the spirit of knight-errantry was dominant, a spirit which in certain fine men is still dominant. I assume that Branicki had told his confessor that his honour obliged him to fight, and since honour must be loved by a soldier more than his life, had found a very docile confessor. This must be so; but I am still astonished by that conscience which convinces itself that it has thus obtained a legitimate absolution.

I do know how the Venetian reasoned. As a Catholic Christian he loved his soul at least as much as the Podstoli loved his, and he would certainly not have gone to fight if he had been sure of being killed, being certain that his soul, on leaving his body, would have gone into eternal fire. Here is the short ejaculation which he made to God mentally: 'I know, O God, that in going to fight I am in mortal sin, because I go to expose myself to an immediate occasion of becoming a murderer; therefore have mercy on my soul, and prevent me from being killed, since, if I were to perish in the act, I know I am not allowed even to pray to you now to exempt me from the eternal pains of hell. Grant me, O God, the time and strength to repent of that sin which, through pride, I am now about to commit wilfully.'

Even this prayer is absurd and contradictory. First, because it is ridiculous for a man to pray to the King of kings for grace when he is aware that his intention of offending him is known. Second, because he has no need to ask to be pardoned for a sin which he has the power not to commit; and from this it follows that, if he commits it, he is twice culpable if he is foolhardy enough to hope for that pardon. Despite this, the Venetian's religion seems to me less irrational than the other's.

The following day a Jesuit came to the convent. He said he was confessor to His Excellency Czartoryski, Bishop of Poznan, and asked for some conversation with the Venetian. In private he told him that he had come in the name of His Excellency to absolve him from the ecclesiastical condemnation which he had incurred by fighting a duel. The Venetian thanked him, and told him that he had not thought himself excommunicated, since he knew that he had not fought a duel. At this point there was a rather lengthy and serious disagreement between him and the Jesuit on the question of whether he had fought a duel or not. This would not readily have been concluded if the Jesuit had not thought out a compromise which did not displease the supposed ex-communicate. This is the formula with which he confessed his fault: 'If, despite the fact that I do not think it a duel, my conflict with the Grand Butler to the Crown was really a duel, I confess it, I repent of it, and I ask Holy Mother Church for absolution from my sin, and my restoration to the communion of the faithful.' Once he had said that, the wise father absolved him and went away. The Venetian for good reasons communicated this fact by letter to the Prince Palatine of Russia. He was anxious that his affair should not be acknowledged to be a duel; and in fact it did not answer to all the requirements.

Meanwhile, the surgeon was not happy with the wound's progress. It was black, he did not like the suppuration, the arm was swollen, and he thought that gangrene was imminent. Five days after he had removed the bandages, he said plainly that he would have to resort to amputating the hand. At the same instant two surgeons arrived from the Court, and after a careful examination they decided that amputation was essential. '*Vous consentirez donc, Monsieur,*' the surgeon, who was French, said to the Venetian who, after fasting five days, was worn out by hunger, '*à vous laisser couper la main, nous ferons cela avec une adresse étonnante, et cela ne sera pas long; en deux minutes vous serez servi.*' '*Monsieur,*' the sick man replied, '*je n'y consens pas.*' '*Et pourquoi, s'il vous plaît?*' said the other, to which the reply was: '*Par ce que je veux garder ma main et personne ne peut y trouver rien a redire, puisque je suis son maître souverain.*'

SURGEON: *Mais, Monsieur, la cancrène va s'y mettre.*
VENETIAN: *Y est elle?*
SURGEON: *Pas encore, mais elle est imminente.*
VENETIAN: *Fort bien. Je veux la voir; j'en suis curieux. Nous parlerons de ceci après son apparition.*
SURGEON: *Ce sera trop tard.*

VENETIAN: *Pourquoi?*

SURGEON: *Par ce que ses progrès sont extremement rapides, et il sera pour lors necessaire de vous couper le bras.*

VENETIAN: *Très bien. Vous me couperez le bras; mais en attendant remettez moi mes bandeaux, et allez vous en.*

[SURGEON: Please give your permission, sir, for your hand to be amputated. We shall perform this operation with a skill that will amaze you, and it won't take long, just two minutes.

VENETIAN: No sir, I do not give my permission.

SURGEON: Please tell me why.

VENETIAN: Because I want to hold on to my hand, and there is no one who can oppose that, since I am its sovereign lord.

SURGEON: But the gangrene...

VENETIAN: Where is it?

SURGEON: It is imminent.

VENETIAN: Very well. And meanwhile I want to see it. I am very curious about it. We shall talk about amputating the hand once the gangrene has appeared.

SURGEON: That will be too late.

VENETIAN: Why?

SURGEON: Because it progresses very rapidly, and then it would be necessary to amputate your arm.

VENETIAN: Excellent. You will amputate my arm. Meanwhile, please replace my bandages and go away.]

Two hours later he learnt from Prince Czartoryski that the King had said he was a fool not to have had his hand amputated, because he would now have to have his arm amputated. He replied to the Prince (after asking him to thank the King) that he did not know what he would do with his arm without his hand. Therefore he begged to be pardoned if he could not make up his mind to have his hand amputated before he had seen the gangrene, but that, as soon as he had seen it, he would not oppose the amputation of his arm. The three surgeons came that evening, ready to perform the operation, and for that reason looking happy and victorious. Once the bandages were removed it was clear that the wound was nice and clean. This perplexed them. The most shrewd one, who was a Pole, maintained that he must have made a vow to some saint. In three weeks the Venetian went out with his arm in a sling, and having lost a lot of weight; but he was well. It was Easter Day.

After he had performed his Easter duties, he went to the Court to kiss the royal hand, but he did not find His Majesty there. Learning that the King was in the home of Prince Oginski, he went there, and when he saw the King he kissed his royal right hand, with one knee bent to the ground. The King raised him up and enquired after that rheumatism which forced him to have his arm in a sling; then, without giving him time to answer, he added: 'I advise you to avoid in the future all occasions of contracting such an illness, because it can be fatal.' The other replied with silence and with a bowed head. Then he went to visit the Podstoli in his apartment in the Grand Chamberlain's house, and he saw how everyone in the antechamber was astonished when he asked to be announced. A Polish official went away timidly. He was quite certain that the Venetian would not be admitted, but he was wrong. He came back, and ordered a servant to throw the doors open, and the Venetian was admitted. The Podstoli was lying down, and he looked tired, but he extended his hand courteously. The other went to him, took his hand, and was obliged to kiss it, and said to him: 'I am sorry, sir, that I am visiting Your Excellency first.

I have come to tell you that I acknowledge that I have been a thousand times more honoured by you than offended, and I ask your pardon that on St Casimir's Day I was unable to disguise that feeling which caused your present indisposition. I ask you to honour me in future with your favour and your protection.' His first statement was a lie, but all the others were the truth, and expressed his true desires. The Podstoli answered: '*Je suis charmé de vous voir, Monsieur; je vous demande pour le tems a venir votre amitié; je crois d'avoir assez bien pajé de ma personne pour la mériter. Je vous prie de vous assoir. Qu'on porte à Monsieur du chocolat.*' ['I am pleased to see you, sir. I ask you for your friendship in times to come. I believe that I have given you enough satisfaction with my person to have earned it. Please sit down. Bring this gentleman some chocolate.']

They talked on various matters tête à tête, but only for a short time. In less than a quarter of an hour more than ten gentlemen's coaches came to that house. They had heard that the Venetian had left the Oginski palace and ordered his coachman to take him to the Podstoli, and they had come there curious to know and see what consequences would follow from a visit which everyone thought was strange and overbold. They all came in and were glad to see that those two were clearly completely reconciled. In all respects the Venetian owed the Podstoli that visit, and yet he would not have dared to pay it alone if the Podstoli had not been sending a servant every day without fail to enquire after his health.

The Venetian's fourth visit was paid to that honourable old man Bielinski, Grand Marshal to the Crown. He approached him and kissed his hand. The great man asked him if he had been to see the King. 'You owe your life to His Majesty,' he said, 'since, if he had not persuaded me to pardon you,

I should have condemned you to death.' The Venetian, although he was not convinced by this, knew enough to bow his head and remain silent.

He spent two months in Warsaw after these events, honoured wherever he went. But he was not easy in his mind. He had refused many deceitful invitations which would have resulted in blood being shed, and he had many enemies and good reason to fear nocturnal ambushes. Several anonymous letters had been sent to the King, and to many important people, showing the poor Venetian in the most abominable light. They represented him as an exile not only from his homeland, but from almost all the countries of Europe: from one for robbing banks, from another for treachery, for theft, for infamous acts of wickedness, and from his homeland for actions which were so iniquitous that they could not be mentioned. These were all calumnies, but do not calumnies have the same effect as accusations which are based on the truth? They may possibly be shown to be unjustified and so dispelled, it is true; but everyone knows how hard it is to do this. Everyone knows that a wretch who has been calumniated never comes through his purgatory of self-justification without continuing to bear the indelible stain of the false accusation. The only wise thing to do, for him who has been persecuted by envy, is to have a change of scenery. *Vir fugiens denuo pugnabit.*[12] Yet it is hard to go away, and leave the field free for the wicked, and allow the guilty to obtain the victory. That is all true; but it is what he has to do who has not foreseen that it is always dangerous to arouse envy, and that he who has aroused it often has to do penance for it. However, one should not therefore abandon virtue for fear of arousing envy. *Invidiam placare paras virtute relicta? Contemnere miser. Vitanda est improba Siren desidia.*[13]

55

The Venetian decided to go and see Podolia, Volhynia, Pokucie, and those Polish parts of Russia which, under another name, live under the discipline of a sceptre which is wiser than the old one. This tour occupied him for three months. He did not spend much on lodging, for always and everywhere he went he was received with great generosity by those great men who, loathing the new system, kept themselves far from the Court. They were punished by the Empress of Russia for their indocility when they dared to oppose her wishes in the Diet. If the Venetian had not seen those lands, he would have had little acquaintance with ancient Poland.

When his arm had recovered all its strength, he returned to Warsaw. He saw the Podstoli, now fit once more. He was coming out of his house, but did not invite the Venetian to go to Court with him. He dined with Princess Lubomirska, and found himself at table with the King, who is her cousin, but he did not have the honour of hearing the royal voice addressed to him. The Prince Palatine of Russia did not again offer him that apartment which he had generously had furnished for him with great splendour. '*Denigratum est aurum*,'[14] he said, and he foresaw what was about to happen to him.

That same adjutant-general who had been present at the duel came to command him in the name of His Majesty to leave the jurisdiction of Warsaw within eight days. The Venetian wrote to Prince Adam Czartoryski a letter of complaint in which he pointed out the injustice of the message which His Majesty had conveyed to him; but Prince Adam replied only with these three words: *Invitus invitum dimitto.*[15] He wrote then to Count Moscynski, whose face had been cut by Biszewski, and who was always by the King's side. He wrote to him to say that he could not obey, since he had many debts, and as a man of honour he had to think about paying them before departing. Count Moscynski rushed in person to his house to find out what his debts amounted to. Once he was informed of this in writing, he left him, after having told him that there were three letters written against him anonymously which had brought about his ruin.

I cannot decide which of the two merits the greater reproof – the coward who writes an anonymous letter against anyone, or the imprudent person who, by paying attention to it, enables the treacherous writer of the letter to achieve his aim. Poisons, knives, secret snares would never have harmed anyone if they had not found people to use them to bad effect. In short, the writer of an anonymous letter is always a traitor, even if the result of that letter happens to be good.

This generous Count Moscynski came in person during the following days to the house where the Venetian was living, and gave him a thousand sequins and wished him bon voyage. With part of this money he paid all his creditors, whose receipts he sent to that noble man, and then he departed for Breslau, the capital of Silesia, where he stayed for eight days, during which he enjoyed the learned conversation and the hospitality of Abbot Bastiani, a Venetian, who held a very distinguished post in the cathedral and a very large prebend.

From Breslau he went on to Dresden, and then to the fair in Lipsia, and then to Prague, and to Vienna, where a very strange event occurred, the account of which, if someone well-informed about the details were to write it, would result, to the punishment of its readers, in a small volume little different from this one.

The Venetian ambassador, who for political reasons did not think he ought to receive the Venetian in his house, had the kindness to save him with two words which he deliberately let slip when he found himself with Prince Kaunitz. That ambassador was always a great man, and today he is very great. On that occasion the implacable Schrattenbach suffered a rebuttal. From Vienna he went to Bavaria, and then to Augusta, where he stayed until he heard that Princess Lubomirska, née Czartoryska, would be at Spa in the month of August. The Venetian set off in that direction, but stopped in the Palatinate and the Württemberg as a result of several adventures, and for one day in Cologne on the left bank of the Rhine to conclude an affair which was close to his heart, and which, because it concerns the duel, ought not to be passed over in silence.

While the Venetian was in Dresden a month after his departure from Poland, he read in the Cologne gazette an article about Warsaw, and found there the story of his dismissal from the Court, written in a style and with certain circumstances which displeased him considerably. All the gazettes put together make up the whole history of the world, and those readers who have no precise knowledge of things but wish to be informed about everything (and they are the majority), go along with what is reported. They think that those people who are commended to them are heroes, and they have a very bad impression of those who are represented as unjust and fraudulent, and since they have no information to the contrary, those impressions which they believe to reflect the truth remain fixed in their memories.

It is not surprising therefore that the poor Venetian was annoyed at finding himself depicted unfairly in that gazette, and surrounded with such lies: he thought it was unjust that someone who wished to be remembered should appear to the world in that light. He would not have been offended if he had read that a general official had dismissed him from the Court by order of the King, and not from the whole of Poland, and not that this happened after the monarch was informed of his true name, and of the false qualities which had been attributed to him, because of which he had appeared to the Court as a very different person from what he was. These outrageous lies were imprinted on the Venetian's mind, and he made a silent resolution to go at his leisure and disabuse the imprudent hack.

So when he came to Cologne in the middle of July, a little less than a year after his departure from the Court in Warsaw, he had the house of the hack, his panegyrist, pointed out to him. Then he went to his inn, had the horses harnessed to his carriage, and departed, taking the Juliers road, which leads to Aix-la-Chapelle; but once outside the city, he ordered his servant to stop and wait there, and he returned to the city alone and on foot. In the city he paid a visit to Monsieur Jacquier, a French hack journalist who lived there. A servant showed him into the room where he was alone, putting his gazette together. The Venetian entered brusquely, closed the door and bolted it, brandished a big stick which he held in his right hand, and drew a pistol from his pocket with his left hand. He approached the hack, who had risen from his seat and stood there trembling.

'If you make any noise, you're dead,' said the Venetian. 'Listen to me, and do immediately what I order you to do, because I am in a hurry. And be careful not to lie, or your life will pay for it.' Having said this, he presented his gazette to the man, who did not even blink, and showing him the article on Warsaw, ordered him to read it clearly. Once he had cast his eyes on it, he tried to speak, but the Venetian raised his stick: 'Read it,' he said, 'and do not speak except to reply to me with the truth, if you wish me to spare your life.' He read the whole article through, but with a voice so strangely trembling one moment, then fading, then sighing, that the good Venetian felt himself all of a sudden struck by a feeling of pity, and with such an urge to laugh that he could scarcely restrain an outburst. When he had finished reading, the Venetian said to him, 'Show me your source for this story, and know that I am the man whom you have defamed in this gazette.' He fell down onto his knees and, admitting he had been unwise, said that he had drawn the article from a letter from Warsaw. The other replied, 'If, unfortunately for you, that letter is not to be found in this room, then you are a dead man.' And he held the pistol to his breast. 'Yes, sir,' he said, falling down with his arms opened wide, 'it should be here in this room, and I'll try to find it straight away.' 'Quick, find it.' He got up and, with the Venetian at his side, he started to seek out packages on the shelves and skim through them. But suddenly he went pale, started to sweat, and let himself fall into a chair. The Venetian found himself in a bit of a fix, and almost regretted his action, but remained firm and waited without speaking for the wretch to come round. He did come round, he found the letter, the Venetian read it, did not recognise either the name or the handwriting, put it in his pocket, and then ordered the hack to write, at his dictation, an article which he made him promise (a promise which he did keep) to include it without alteration in the next issue. He made him copy it, and kept the copy for himself. He then commanded him to go with him, and did not allow him to go and fetch a cape (which he said he had in another room) to protect himself from the pouring rain. He made him conduct him to his carriage and, having warned him to take great care to avoid a second visit, he gave him two louis, and so the affair was concluded. The hack was as good as his word, but the Venetian was left not entirely satisfied: he would never know the identity of that person who, with a name quite unknown, had written those lies. The hack deserved a good beating, simply because he believed that showing the letter was enough to prove him innocent; but the Venetian, who was excellent at ruminating revenge, was weak when it came to the point of carrying it out, because it was his good fortune to be subject to feelings of pity. Pity is an heroic feeling, and it is a shame that, when it is examined thoughtfully, it can be seen to proceed from a weakness in the mind. Today this man has got to the stage that there is no adversity on earth that can perplex him except for a brief instant. He concentrates on sympathising with him who condemns him, on blaming him who puts his trust in men, in scorning the proud, and in wishing to be helpful to all those who have harmed him. This is a sublime and heroic revenge, even if it is accompanied by a touch of pride, as I am afraid it is. There are few people in his homeland whom he respects, but he is glad to see that those few are furnished with that true merit which only the eyes of the wise can discern. It is their approval alone which he seeks and, sickened by the world, he awaits, without either desiring it or fearing it, the dissolution of his body, while endeavouring to keep it peaceful and healthy. It is not the least of his defects that he wishes to make certain worldly truths known to people who, too predisposed in their own favour, are not open to instruction, or cannot bear that it should issue from someone whom they regard as an inferior. When the Venetian has become truly wise, if he is granted the time to do that, then, happy with what he knows, and always willing to learn from those who have more experience than he, he will allow everyone to believe what he wants to, and he will not try to force the truth onto those who are recalcitrant and are unwilling to divest themselves of those false notions and bits of information which they cherish. Men are by nature such that they cannot bring themselves to learn anything from those who wish to force instruction on them; and they are in the right, just as the others are in the wrong.

But it is time to conclude. The Venetian went to Spa, then to Paris, where he remained for three months in an effort to convince the King of Poland of the falsity of an anonymous letter, then to Spain, where he suffered very great misfortunes, and secret attempts on his life which would not have happened if he had been wise. Constantly bearing up, however, he overcame all difficulties and, leaving that kingdom behind, he crossed over Languedoc, Provence, and Piedmont. He then went on to write the confutation of a malevolent history[16] in a country which he would not have left if a minister of state had not stirred him and aroused in him the ambition to take part in the Russian expedition on the sea against the King of the Turks. He was in Leghorn where, as his destiny would have it, Count Alexei Orlov would not accept him under the conditions he set. Then he went to Naples, and then he spent a year in Rome, and then he went on to Florence. But at the end of six months he had to leave by a sovereign command, and for reasons which must have been legitimate, because it is a wise person who knows them, but which the Venetian was not worthy to know, or to imagine. From Tuscany he went to Bologna, where he stayed for nine months, and then to Ancona in order to go overseas. He was two years in Trieste, and was able to return towards the end of the year 1774, through the sovereign clemency of his homeland. If he had been worthy of that favour, he would easily have been able to make a living there.

I hope that this portion of the Venetian's history will serve to open the eyes of those who long for him to write it all. They should know that, if he were disposed to gratify them, he could never bring himself to do it in any style or with any method different from those exemplified in this account. Views, reflections, digressions, minute circumstances, critical observations, dialogues, soliloquies – all of them would have to suffer from a pen which is not, and does not wish to be, restrained, since it certainly will not waste ink spreading wickedness or lies which are liable to sully the social decencies, to render the feelings of a humble subject suspect, or to bring once more into doubt the right and proper thoughts of the Christian man.

NOTES

1. Epigraph: 'Control your anger; for unless it has to obey, it will command; put a bridle on it, and curb it with chains.'

2. Robert-François Damiens (1715–57) made an unsuccessful attempt to assassinate King Louis XV of France. He was tortured and put to death in the Place de Grève.

3. Historic region and former duchy, in Latvia, between the Baltic Sea and the Western Dvina River. Mitau was the Russian name of the Latvian city of Jelgava.

4. Baldassare Galuppi (1706–85), nicknamed 'Buranello' because of his origin on the island of Burano near Venice, was one of the most prolific and influential composers of his generation.

5. Tressette is a classic Italian card-game, still very popular today.

6. Literally.

7. 'The sweet flavours will turn to bile, and the thick phlegm will upset the stomach. Do you see how every guest rises pale from the unhealthy meal? Indeed the body, overburdened with yesterday's excesses, drags the mind also down at the same time, and fastens a particle of the divine spirit to the earth.' (Horace, *Satires*, II, 2, 75–9)

8. 'There is a great difference between *cavalier* in French and *cavaliere* in Italian. I ask pardon of those who do not need this warning.' (Casanova's note). He appears to be distinguishing the sense of 'man of honour' from a mere honorific.

9. The wounded are afflicted by hunger.

10. Provisionally.

11. At the point of death.

12. The man who flees will live to fight again.

13. 'Do you hope to placate envy by abandoning virtue? Wretch, you will be despised. You must avoid that wicked Siren, sloth.' (Horace, *Satires*, II, 3, 13–5)

14. Gold is despised.

15. I dismiss unwillingly you who are unwilling to go.

16. *The History of the Venetian Government* by Amelot de la Hussaie, 1769. The country Casanova refers to is Switzerland.

The Duel

Extract from Casanova's *Memoirs*

My duel with Branicki. Journey to Leopol[1] and return to Warsaw. I receive the King's command to leave. My departure with the unknown woman.

Reflecting on this unfortunate event[2] when I was at home, I concluded that Branicki had not been impolite in getting into Tomatis' coach. He had acted in an unceremonious way; but he would have done the same thing if Tomatis had been his close friend. He might have foreseen some jealousy on the part of the Italian, but he could not have foreseen opposition of that kind from Tomatis; if he had foreseen it, he would not have exposed himself to the affront unless he was determined to kill whoever gave it to him. The moment he received it, he was naturally roused to vengeance, and he took that vengeance which came into his head – a box on the ear! It was too much, but it was less than if he had killed him. Then it would have been said that he had murdered him, despite the fact that Tomatis also had a sword, for Branicki's servants would not have given him time to draw it from its scabbard.

Nevertheless, I believe that Tomatis should have killed the servant, even at the risk of his own life. That required less courage than he had displayed in ordering the Podstoli to the Crown to get out of his coach. I considered Tomatis much at fault in not foreseeing that Branicki would respond to the affront with violence, and consequently in not being on his guard at the moment when Branicki suffered the affront. The real fault, in my opinion, was Madame Gattai's: she should never have entered the coach on the Podstoli's arm.

The next day, this was being talked about everywhere. Tomatis stayed indoors for eight days, asking the King and all his patrons for a vengeance which he was quite unable to obtain. Even the King did not know what kind of satisfaction he could gain for the foreigner, for Branicki maintained that he had given insult for insult. Tomatis told me in confidence that he would have found some means of avenging himself, if that had not been too costly for him. For the two performances he had disbursed forty thousand sequins, which he would assuredly have lost if, by taking vengeance, he had put himself into the position of having to leave the kingdom. The only thing that consoled him was that those marks of favour with which the great families to which he was attached honoured him redoubled, and the King himself often spoke in his favour at the theatre, at table, and on walks.

Only Madame Binetti rejoiced at this incident, and was triumphant. When I went to see her, she teased me by expressing her sympathy for the misfortune (as she called it) which had overtaken my friend. She irritated me; but I could not be certain that Branicki had only acted as he had because he had been encouraged by her, or make out whether she wanted the same thing to happen to me. However, even if I had been certain, I would have made light of it, since the Podstoli could not do me any harm or any good. I never saw him, I had never spoken to him, and so I could not give him cause. I did not see him even in the company of the King, for he was never there at the same hour as I was; and he never came to the palace of the Prince Palatine, not even in the King's retinue when he came to dine there. Branicki was a gentleman whom the whole nation loathed, because he was of the Russian party, a great supporter of the dissidents, and enemy of all those who did not wish to bow their necks to the yoke to which Russia wished to subject their ancient constitution. The King liked him because of their old friendship, because he had certain obligations to him, and also for political reasons. This monarch had to sit on the fence, since he had Russia to fear if he came out against the system which had already been agreed, just as he had his nation to fear if he acted openly.

I was living an exemplary life – no love affairs, no gambling. I was working for the King, hoping to become his secretary. I paid court to the Princess Palatine, who liked my company, and I played tressette with the Palatine against any two others who chanced to be there. On the 4th of March, the vigil of St Casimir (which was the name of the Grand Chamberlain, the elder brother of the King), there was a great feast at Court, and I was there. After dinner the King asked me if I was going to the play that evening. For the first time a play was to be put on in the Polish language. Everyone else was intrigued by this novelty, but I was indifferent to it, since I had no Polish; and I told the King so.

'That doesn't matter. Come anyway. Come in my box.'

When he said that, I bowed my head and obeyed. I stood behind his chair. After the second act there was a ballet in which Madame Casacci, a Piedmontese dancer, performed so well that the King clapped his hands. This was an extraordinary mark of favour. I did not know this dancer except by sight; I had never spoken to her; she was not without talent; and her great friend was Count Poninski who, every time that I went to dine with him, reproached me for visiting other dancers, yet never Madame Casacci, where, nevertheless, one was well-received. After the ballet it occurred to me to leave the King's box and visit Madame Casacci in her dressing-room to compliment her on the well-merited applause which the King had given her. I passed by the open door of Madame Binetti's dressing-room, which was open, and I paused for a moment. Count Branicki, who was said to be her lover, went in and I, after bowing to him, went away. I paid a visit to Madame Casacci who, astonished to see me for the first time, reproached me in a kindly way. I paid her my compliments, I promised to visit her, and I embraced her. At the very instant we embraced, Count Branicki entered; it was no more than a minute since I had left him with Madame Binetti; he had clearly followed me; but why? To provoke a quarrel. He wanted one with me. With him was Lieutenant-Colonel Biszewski, of his regiment. When he appeared, I rose, out of politeness and also in order to take my leave; but he stopped me by saying:

'I have come in, sir, at the wrong time for you. I think you are in love with this lady.'

'Of course, sir. Does not Your Excellency find her lovable?'

'Lovable, yes. But, what is more, I tell you that I love her, and that I am not the kind of man to suffer rivals.'

'Well, well! Now that I know that, I shall not love her any more.'

'You give way to me then?'

'Willingly. Everyone has to give way to a gentleman like yourself.'

'That is all very well, but a man who gives way *f… le camp.*'

'That is a little strong.'

As I said this, I went out, looking at him and showing him the hilt of my sword. Three or four officers, who happened to be there, witnessed the whole incident. I had not gone four steps away from the dressing-room when I heard myself honoured with the title of 'Venetian coward'; I turned and said to him that outside the theatre a Venetian coward might well kill a brave Pole, and I went down the main staircase leading to the door which gives onto the street. I waited there for a quarter of an hour, hoping to see him come out with his sword in his hand, since I was not held back, as Tomatis was, by the fear of losing forty thousand sequins. But when he did not come, and I was chilled through, I called my servants, had my carriage brought, and went to the home of the Prince Palatine of Russia, where the King himself had said that he would dine.

When I was alone in my carriage and my first impulse had calmed down somewhat, I was pleased with myself for having resisted the temptation to violence, and not having drawn my sword in Madame Casacci's dressing-room. And I realised also that I was glad that my insulter had not come down, for he had Biszewski with him, armed with a sabre, and he would have murdered me. The Poles, although generally quite civilised these days, still keep many of their old tendencies. They are still Sarmatians and Dacians at table, in war, and in that passion which they call friendship. They never understand that one man is enough for another man, and that it is not right to come in a troop and cut the throat of someone who is by himself, and only wishes to meet one of them. I saw clearly that Branicki had followed me, encouraged by Madame Binetti, with the intention of treating me as he had treated Tomatis. I had not been given a box on the ear, but something that was almost the equivalent. Three officers could witness that he had sent me packing, and I recognised that I had been dishonoured. It was not in my nature to endure such a stigma, and I felt that I must come to some decision, but I did not know what. I must have complete satisfaction, and I thought about procuring it by some moderate means, by running with the hare and hunting with the hounds. I came to the home of the King's uncle, Prince Czartoryski, Palatine of Russia, determined to tell the King everything, and leave it to His Majesty to oblige Branicki to ask my pardon.

When the Palatine saw me, he reproached me for keeping him waiting a little, and then we sat down, as always, to a game of tressette. I was his partner. When we had lost two games, he blamed it on me, and asked me what I was thinking of.

'My mind was miles away, sir.'

'When one is playing tressette,' he responded, 'with an honest man who wishes to enjoy the game, then it is not allowed to have one's mind miles away.'

Saying this, the Prince threw the cards onto the table, arose, and went for a walk about the room. I stood there, quite nonplussed, and then I went to the fireplace, thinking that the King could not be long. Half an hour later, the chamberlain Pernigotti came and told the Prince that the King could not come. This announcement pierced me to the quick, but I dissimulated my feelings. The order to serve was given, and I took my usual place by the side of the Palatine. There were eighteen or twenty of us at the table. The Palatine was annoyed with me. I did not eat. Halfway through the meal, Prince Kaspr Lubomirski, lieutenant-general in the service of Russia, arrived and sat at the other end of the table, opposite me. The moment he saw me, he expressed in a loud voice his sympathy over what had happened to me.

'I am sorry for you,' he said. 'Branicki was drunk, and an honest man cannot receive an affront from a man who is drunk.'

'So what's happened, what's happened?'

That is what everyone wanted to know. I said nothing. They questioned Lubomirski, and he said that since I was silent he must stay silent too. So the Palatine brightened up, and asked me kindly what had happened between me and Branicki.

'I shall give you an exact account of everything, sir, in private, when we have eaten.'

Then talk went on to unimportant matters, until the end of the meal. When we arose, the Palatine went to stand by the small door where he was in the habit of withdrawing, and I followed him. In five or six minutes I had told him everything. He sighed. He expressed his sympathy for me and told me it was not surprising that I had not had my wits about me while we were playing cards.

'I should like Your Excellency's advice.'

'I do not give advice in matters like this, where one should do much or nothing.'

After saying these wise words, he went to his apartment. So I took my pelisse, got into my carriage, and went home. I went to bed, and my constitution is so good that I slept for six hours. At five in the morning, sitting up in bed, I thought about what action I should take. *Much or nothing.* I immediately rejected *nothing.* Therefore I had to choose from *much.* I could think of only one way: kill Branicki, or oblige him to kill me, if he wished to honour me with a duel; and if he had tormented me without being willing to fight, I must murder him, doing it with care, and even risking my head on the scaffold for it. I made my mind up, and I thought I should begin by proposing a duel four leagues from Warsaw, since the jurisdiction ran for four leagues all round, and inside it duels were forbidden under penalty of death. So I wrote to him this letter, which I am now copying from the original which I have kept.

Today, 5 March 1766, at 5 o'clock in the morning. Your Excellency, at the theatre yesterday evening you offended me out of sheer light-heartedness, without having any reason or right to act towards me in such a way. That being the case, I judge, Your Excellency, that you hate me and consequently desire to remove me from the land of the living. I am able and willing to satisfy you. May it please Your

Excellency to take me with you in your carriage, and to conduct me to a place where my death may not cause you to violate the laws of Poland, and where I may enjoy the same advantage, if with God's help I succeed in killing you. I should not make this proposal to you, Your Excellency, if I did not know how magnanimous you are.

I have the honour to be Your Excellency's very humble and obedient servant,

Casanova

I sent this letter by my servant one hour before daybreak to the palace where Branicki's apartment adjoined that of the King. I told the servant to give it only into his hands, and that, if he was asleep, he should wait until he awakened in order to receive a response. I only had to wait a quarter of an hour. Here is a copy of what he wrote:

Sir,

I accept your proposal, but beg you to have the goodness, sir, to inform me when I shall have the honour of seeing you. I am truly, sir, your most humble and obedient servant,

Branicki Podstoli

Pleased with my good fortune, I replied immediately that I would be with him the next day at six o'clock in the morning, to go with him where we could finish the quarrel in a safe place. He replied by asking me to name the weapons and the place, and saying it must all be settled on that day. So I told him the length of my sword, which was thirty-two inches, and said that it was up to him to choose the place, provided that it was outside the jurisdiction. Straight away he replied with this letter, which was the last:

I should be grateful, sir, if you would take the trouble to come and see me immediately. I am sending my carriage to you for that purpose. I have the honour to be etc.

I replied with just four lines to tell him that, having a great deal to do, I was obliged to spend the day at home, and that, having decided that I would only call upon him if it was for the purpose of fighting, he must excuse me if I returned his carriage.

An hour later he arrived at my house, entered my chamber, leaving his attendants outside and sending out three or four people who were there talking with me. He bolted the door and sat on my bed, where I was sitting up for the greater ease in writing. Not knowing what he wanted to say, I seized two pocket pistols which I had on my bedside table.

'I have not come here to kill you, but to tell you that when I accept a challenge to fight, I never put it off to the next day. So we will fight today or not at all.'

'I cannot fight today. It is Wednesday, the day for the post, and I have something which I must finish and send to the King.'

'You can send it after we have fought. You won't be killed, believe me. And if you are, the King will pardon you. A dead man cannot suffer any reproach.'

'I have also my will to write.'

'A will now! You are afraid of dying! Dismiss this fear. You can make your will fifty years from now.'

'But what is the problem for Your Excellency in delaying our duel until tomorrow?'

'I don't want to be trapped. Tomorrow we shall both be put under arrest by order of the King.'

'That's not possible. Unless you intend to tell him of it?'

'I intend to? You make me laugh. I'm up to your tricks. You will not have challenged me in vain. I wish to give you satisfaction, but it must be today or never.'

'Very well. This duel matters too much to me to give you a pretext for not fighting it. Come to fetch me after lunch, for I need all my strength.'

'With pleasure. For myself, I prefer to eat afterwards. But by the way, what is this business of the length of your sword? I wish to fight with pistols. I do not fight with the sword against someone I do not know.'

'What do you mean "you do not know"? I can give you in Warsaw twenty witnesses to say that I am not a fencing-master. I don't wish to fight with pistols, and you cannot oblige me to, for you have given me the choice of weapons, and I have your letter to prove it.'

'Well, strictly you are right, for I know that I gave you the choice. But you are too gallant to refuse to fight with pistols, if I assure you that this would please me. It is the least you can do for me. I can tell you, too, that with pistols we shall be less at risk, for people usually miss, and if I miss you, I promise you that we will then fight with swords as much as you like. Are you willing to give me this pleasure?'

'I like your way of speaking, because it shows some wit. I even feel myself inclined to give you this barbarous pleasure, and with a little effort I can find it in me to share it with you. I therefore accept the new arrangements for our duel under the following precise conditions. You will come with two pistols which you will make sure are loaded in my presence, and I shall have the choice between them. But if we miss each other, we shall fight with swords until the first blood is shed, and no longer; but only if that suits you, because I am ready to fight to the death. You will come and fetch me at three o'clock, and we shall go where we will be safe from the law.'

'Very well. You are a kind man. Let me embrace you. Give me your word of honour that you will say nothing to anyone, or we will be arrested.'

'Why do you think I would expose myself to that risk, when I would travel many leagues on foot to be worthy of the honour that you wish to do me?'

'All the better. Everything has been said. Goodbye until three o'clock.'

This is a faithful report of what was said, as everyone has known for thirty-two years. As soon as this brave braggart had left me, I put all the papers which were for the King into a packet which I sealed, and sent for the dancer Campioni, who had my entire confidence.

'Here is a packet,' I said to him, 'which you will give back to me this evening if I live, and which you will take to the King if I am dead. You can guess what all this is about, but remember that if you speak of it I shall be dishonoured, and apart from that, I declare that you will have no more fierce enemy in the world than myself.'

'I understand perfectly. If I revealed the affair to those who would certainly prevent it, people would say that you yourself had encouraged me to do this. I want you to come out of this with honour. The only advice I dare give you is not to spare your adversary, even if he is the lord of all. Such an indulgence might cost you your life.'

'I know that from experience.'

I ordered a choice dinner, and I sent to the Court for some excellent Burgundy. Campioni dined with me. The two young Counts of Mniszech, with their tutor, the Swiss Bertrand, paid me a visit while I was at table, and witnessed my good appetite and extraordinary gaiety. At a quarter to three I asked them all to leave me alone, and I went to the window to be ready to go down the moment that the Podstoli arrived at my door.

I saw him arrive in a berlin drawn by six horses, preceded by two grooms on horseback, leading two saddled horses, two hussars, and two aides-de-camp. There were four mounted servants behind the carriage. He stopped at my door, I came down quickly from the third floor, and I saw he was accompanied by a lieutenant-general and by a chasseur who was seated at the front. The door of the carriage opened, the lieutenant-general gave me his place and went to sit at the front by the chasseur. With one foot on the step of the carriage, I turned to my servants and ordered them not to follow me but to stay at home and await my orders. The Podstoli told me that I might have need of them, and I answered that if I had as many as he, I would bring them, but since I only had those two wretches, I preferred to put myself in his hands, being certain that he would see I was looked after, if there was any need. He replied that he would have more care of me than of himself, and gave me his hand on it. I sat down, and away we went. He must have arranged this beforehand, because no one spoke a word. It would have seemed silly to ask where we were going. There are times when a man must be circumspect. The Podstoli did not speak, so I thought it was up to me to make some inconsequential remarks.

'Do you intend, sir, to spend the spring and summer in Warsaw?'

'I was intending to, yesterday. But you may prevent me.'

'I hope I shall not upset any of your plans.'

'Have you ever served as a soldier?'

'Yes, I have. But may I ask why Your Excellency asks me this question? Because…'

'No reason, no reason. I asked it just for something to say.'

After half an hour the carriage stopped at the gate of a beautiful garden. We got out and, followed by the Podstoli's whole entourage, we went to a green arbour (which was not green on the 5th of March) with a stone table at one end of it. The chasseur placed two pistols, about a foot and a half long, on the table, and took from his pocket a bag of powder and a pair of scales. He unscrewed the pistols, weighed out the powder and the balls, charged the pistols, screwed them up again tightly, and laid them crosswise on the table. Branicki boldly invited me to choose. The lieutenant-general asked him in a loud voice if this was to be a duel.

'Yes.'

'You cannot fight here: you are in the jurisdiction.'

'That doesn't matter.'

'It matters a great deal, and I must not be a witness to it. I am on guard duty at the palace, and you have taken me by surprise.'

'Be silent. I am responsible for it all, and I owe this gentleman satisfaction.'

'Monsieur Casanova, you cannot fight here.'

'Then why have I been brought here? I will defend myself anywhere, even in church.'

'Lay the matter before the King, and I assure you of his favourable opinion.'

'I shall do so willingly, if His Excellency will only tell me in your presence that he is sorry for what happened yesterday between him and me.'

At this suggestion Branicki scowled at me, and said angrily that he had come there to fight and not to discuss terms. I then said to the general that he could witness that I had done everything in my power to avoid the duel. He withdrew, holding his head in his hands. Branicki urged me to choose.

I threw off my pelisse, and seized the first pistol I came to. Branicki, taking the other, said that he would guarantee on his honour that the weapon which I had in my hand was perfect. I answered that I was about to try it out against his head. At this terrible reply he went pale, threw his sword to one of his attendants, and showed me that his breast was quite bare. I was compelled to do the same – with regret, because my sword was the only weapon I had after my pistol. I showed him my breast too, and I stepped back five or six paces, with the Podstoli doing the same. We could not go any further back. Seeing that he was as steady as I was, with the muzzle of his pistol pointing to the ground, I took off my hat with my left hand, and asked him to honour me by firing first, and put myself on guard. The Podstoli, instead of firing first, lost two or three seconds in drawing himself up and hiding his head behind the butt of his pistol; but the circumstances did not require that I should await his convenience. I fired at him at precisely the same instant as he fired at me, and that was quite clear, for all the people in the neighbouring houses said that they only heard one shot. When I saw him fall, I put my left hand quickly into my pocket, because I knew it was wounded and, throwing my pistol away, I ran towards him. But what was my surprise to find three naked sabres, in the hands of three noble executioners, raised against me! They would have hacked me to pieces in an instant, on my knees as I was, if the Podstoli, in a voice of thunder, had not stopped them in their tracks, crying out:

'Scoundrels! Respect this honest man.'

They drew back, and I went to help him get up, placing my right hand beneath his armpit while the general helped him from the other side. In this way we took him to the inn which was some hundred paces away. He was all bent up as he walked, and he studied me from the side, because he could not understand where the blood, which he saw flowing down my trousers and white stockings, came from.

The moment we got into the inn, the Podstoli threw himself down into a large armchair and stretched out. They unbuttoned him and lifted his shirt up to his stomach, and he saw for himself that he was mortally wounded. My ball had entered his stomach on the right at the seventh rib, and had come out below the last false rib on the left. The two holes were six inches away from each other. The sight was alarming: it looked as though the intestines were pierced, and the man was dead. The Podstoli looked at me, and said:

'You have killed me. Save yourself, or you will lose your head on the scaffold. You are in the jurisdiction, I am an important officer of the Crown, and this is the ribbon of the White Eagle. Save yourself now. And if you have no money, take my purse. Here it is.'

He dropped his heavy purse, but I put it back in his pocket, saying I had no need of it, since if I was guilty of killing him I was going to throw myself at the foot of the throne. I told him I hoped his wound would not be mortal, and that I was in despair because of what he had obliged me to do. I kissed his forehead and went out from the inn, and I saw no carriage, no horses, and no servants. They had all gone to find a physician, a surgeon, priests, relatives, and friends. I found myself alone and unarmed, with the countryside covered in snow, and I did not know the way back to Warsaw. Then in the distance I saw a sledge drawn by two horses. I shouted out, and the peasant stopped. I showed him a ducat, and said:

'Warsaw.'

He heard me, he lifted up a mat, I crawled under it, and he covered me with it to protect me from the splashing mud. He went very fast. After a quarter of an hour Biszewski, Branicki's faithful friend, came towards us at full speed, with a naked sabre in his hand. If he had looked carefully at the sledge, he would have seen my head, which he would have lopped off. When I arrived at Warsaw, I had myself taken to the house of Prince Adam to ask for asylum, but I found no one there. I resolved to take refuge in the Franciscan convent which was a hundred yards away.

I went to the convent door and rang the bell. The porter, a monk without pity, opened the door, saw me covered in blood, presumed that I was trying to save myself from justice, and tried to close the door again. But I did not give him time to do so. A kick in the stomach threw him over, with his legs in the air, and I went in. I shouted for help, some monks came on the scene, and I told them that I wanted asylum, and threatened them if they refused. One of them spoke to me and took me to a poor room rather like a dungeon. I was submissive, knowing that he would change his mind in a quarter of an hour. I asked someone to bring me my servants, who came immediately. Then I sent for a surgeon and for Campioni. But, before they arrived, there came the Palatine of Podlasie, who had never spoken to me but who, having fought a duel in his youth, seized the opportunity to come and tell me all about it, as soon as had heard all about mine. A moment later I saw the arrival of the Palatine of Kalisz, Prince Jablonowski, Prince Sanguszko, and the Palatine of Vilna³, Oginski. They began with great threats to the monks for lodging me like a convict. The monks excused their actions by saying that I had ill-treated the porter. The princes laughed at this, but I did not because of the pain of my wound. I was immediately given two fine rooms.

Branicki's ball had entered my hand by the metacarpus below the forefinger, and had broken the first phalanx. Its force had been weakened by a metal button on my jacket, and by my stomach which it had wounded slightly near the navel. It was necessary to remove this ball which was distressing me considerably. An amateur surgeon, named Gendron, the first who could be found, extracted the ball, after making an incision on the other side of the hand, so that I now had two wounds. While he was performing this painful operation, I told the whole story to the princes, and I dissimulated without difficulty all the anguish which the maladroit surgeon caused me when he introduced the pincers to seize the ball. So great is the power of vanity over the human spirit!

When Gendron had gone, the Prince Palatine's surgeon arrived. He took complete charge of me, and took it upon himself to make sure that the other surgeon was dismissed, saying that he was unqualified. At the same time Prince Lubomirski arrived, the son-in-law of the Prince Palatine of Russia, who astonished us all when he told us everything that had happened immediately after my duel. As soon as Biszewski arrived at Wola, he saw his friend horribly wounded, did not see me there, and went away in a fury, swearing to kill me wherever he found me. He went to the home of Tomatis, who was in company with his mistress, Prince Lubomirski, and Count Moscynski. He asked Tomatis where I was, and when Tomatis answered that he did not know, he discharged his pistol at his head. At this murderous action, Moscynski took hold of him from the side to throw him out of the window, but Biszewski escaped with three slashes of his sabre, one of which gashed Moscynski's face and made him lose three teeth.

'After that,' continued Prince Lubomirski, 'he seized me by my collar, holding a pistol to my throat and threatening me with death if I failed to take him down to the courtyard and his horse, so that he might leave without fearing anything from Tomatis' servants. I did this immediately. Moscynski went home, where he will have to remain for a long time under the care of his doctor, and I went home to witness all the confusion into which your duel has plunged the city. Branicki is said to be dead, and his ulans are on horseback looking everywhere for you: they want to avenge their colonel by killing you. It's a good thing you're here. The Grand Marshal has surrounded the convent with two hundred dragoons, ostensibly in order to make sure he has you imprisoned, but really in order to prevent those madmen breaking into the convent and slaughtering you here. His surgeons say that Branicki is in great danger if the ball has pierced his intestines, but if not, they will answer for his life. They will know tomorrow. He is lodging with the Grand Chamberlain, since he doesn't dare go to his apartment at Court. The King has however been to see him. The general who was present at the duel says that what saved your life was that you threatened to wound Branicki in the head. By trying to safeguard his head he put himself into an awkward posture and so he missed you. Otherwise he would have pierced your heart, for he can fire at the edge of a blade and split the ball in two. The other piece of good luck which you had was in not being seen by Biszewski, who never imagined that you might be under the mat on the sledge.'

'My greatest piece of luck, sir, was that I did not kill Branicki. I was about to be slaughtered on the spot, but he stopped it by a few words, when his friends had already lifted their sabres to strike me. I regret what has happened to Your Highness and the good Count Moscynski. The fact that Tomatis was not killed by the pistol-shot suggests that the pistol was loaded with a blank.'

'That's what I think too.'

At that instant an official from the Palatine of Russia brought me a letter from his master. In it he wrote: 'See what the King has just sent me, and put your mind at rest.' And this is what I read in the letter which the King had written to him, and which I still have: 'Branicki, my dear uncle, is very ill, and my surgeons are with him to give him every help they can; but I have not forgotten Casanova. You may assure him of my favour even if Branicki dies.'

I pressed this letter respectfully to my lips, and I showed it to the noble assembly who were full of admiration for this man who was truly worthy of his crown. I wanted them to leave me, and they left. After they had gone my friend Campioni returned my packet to me and, weeping some fond tears, he congratulated me on the honour which I had obtained from this affair. He had been in the background all this time and had heard all that passed.

The next day there were crowds of visitors, and I was sent purses full of gold from the leaders of those who were opposed to Branicki. The officials who presented me with a purse from this lord or that lady always said to me that, since I was a foreigner, I might be in need of money, and they had, in this belief, taken the liberty of sending me some. I thanked them and refused to accept it. I returned at least four thousand ducats, and was proud of that. Campioni regarded my heroism as ridiculous, and he was right. I repented of it afterwards. The only present I accepted was a dinner for four people which Prince Czartoryski sent me in every day. But I myself did not eat any of it. *Vulnerati fame crucientur* was the favourite saying of my surgeon, a man who would never set the Thames on fire. The wound in my stomach was already festering. What was worse, on the fourth day my arm had swollen and the wound in my hand had gone black. Gangrene was suspected. My surgeons took counsel together and decided that my hand must be amputated. I came across this remarkable news the next morning when I read it in the Court gazette, which was printed during the night after the King had authorised it. It made me laugh. I laughed in the faces of all those who came that morning to express their sympathy, and at the very moment when I was making fun of Count Clary for trying to persuade me to let the operation go ahead, there came in not one surgeon but several.

'Why are there three of you?'

'Because,' said my usual surgeon, 'before proceeding with the amputation I wanted to have the agreement of these experts. We're just about to see what state you are in.'

He removed the dressings, pulled out the seton, and examined the wound, and its colour, and the livid swelling. They discussed it with each other in Polish, and then all three agreed to tell me in Latin that they would amputate my hand that evening. They were all quite happy, and told me that there was nothing to fear, and that by this means I could be quite sure of a good recovery. I replied that I was the lord of my own hand, and that I would never allow them to perform this ridiculous amputation.

'There is gangrene there, and tomorrow it will have got to the arm, and then the arm will have to be amputated.'

'Yes, yes, yes... You will amputate my arm, but as far as I can see there isn't any gangrene.'

'You do not know as much about it as we do.'

'Go away.'

Two hours later began a series of irritating visits from all those whom the surgeons had told of my obstinacy. The Prince Palatine even wrote to me to say that the King was quite amazed by my lack of courage. That was when I wrote to tell the King that I would not know what to do with my arm without my hand, and so I would allow them to amputate my arm, once the gangrene became visible.

The whole Court read my letter. Prince Lubomirski told me that I had been wrong to laugh at those who had my interest at heart, because ultimately it was impossible that the three best surgeons in Warsaw could be deceived over such a simple matter.

'Sir, they are not deceived, but they think they can deceive me.'

'To what end?'

'To do Count Branicki a favour. He is very ill, and he may need this consolation in order to get better.'

'Oh, as far as that goes, you must allow me to disagree.'

'But what will you say when I am found to be right?'

'If that comes about, you will have my admiration, and your steadfastness will bring you many praises. But that day has not yet come.'

'We shall see this evening if the gangrene has attacked the arm, and tomorrow morning I shall have my arm amputated. I give you my word.'

In the evening there were four surgeons who came. They straightened my arm to its full extent, and I could see that it was livid right up to the elbow. But when the dressing was taken off the wound, I could see its edges were red and I could see some matter. I said nothing. Prince Sulkowski and the Abbé Gourel, who was from the Prince Palatine's Court, were present. The four surgeons decided that the arm was infected, it was too late to amputate the hand, and that therefore they would have to amputate the arm by the next morning at the latest. I was tired of arguing, and so I told them to come with the necessary instruments, and I would submit to the operation. They went away very happily to give this news to the Court, to Branicki, and to the Prince Palatine. The next morning, however, I ordered my servant not to let them in, and the story was at an end. I still have my hand.

On Easter Day I went to Mass with my arm in a sling. I did not recover its full use for another eighteen months. It took only twenty-five days to heal. Those who had condemned me found themselves obliged to praise me. My steadfastness brought me great honour, and the surgeons had to admit that they were all either totally ignorant or very imprudent.

But three days after the duel I had another little adventure which I found amusing. A Jesuit came on behalf of the Bishop of Poznan, whose diocese included Warsaw, to speak with me privately. I made everyone leave, and asked him what he wanted.

'I have been delegated by His Excellency (he was one of the Czartoryski family, a brother of the Palatine of Russia) to absolve you from the ecclesiastical condemnation which you have incurred by fighting a duel.'

'I have no need of it, since I am not in that situation. I was attacked, and I defended myself. Please thank the Bishop for me. If however you are willing to absolve me from the sin without my confession, then I shall not object.'

'If you do not confess the sin, then I cannot absolve you. But just do one thing for me: ask me for absolution in case you have fought a duel.'

'With pleasure. If it was a duel, I beg for your absolution, and I beg for nothing from you, if it was not.'

He gave me absolution in the same form. The Jesuits are admirable in finding subterfuges to suit any occasion.

Three days before I went out of doors for the first time, the Grand Marshal to the Crown withdrew the troops from outside the convent. It was Easter Day. I went first to Mass, and then to the Court where the King, extending his hand for me to kiss, let me bend the knee before him. He asked me (it had all been arranged) why I had my arm in a sling, and I replied that I was suffering from rheumatism. He warned me not to have any attacks of it in future. After seeing the King, I told my coachman to take me to where Count Branicki was staying. I thought I owed him a visit. He had been sending a servant every day to find out how I was, and he had returned the sword which I had left on the field of battle. He had to stay in bed for at least six more weeks: his two wounds had had to be reopened because their dressings had caught in them and were preventing his recovery. I owed him a visit. The King had just done him the honour of appointing him Lowczyc, which means Grand Chasseur to the Crown. This office was below that of Podstoli, but it was lucrative. They told him jokingly that the King had only given him that appointment after seeing that he could shoot perfectly well. But on that one day I shot better than he did.

When I entered his antechamber, his officers, his servants, and his chasseurs were surprised to see me. I asked the adjutant to announce me, if his master was receiving. He said nothing in reply, but sighed and went away. He returned a minute later, threw open the doors, and asked me to enter.

Branicki, wearing a dressing-gown of glossy gold, was in bed with his back supported by pillows with rose-coloured ribbons. He was as pale as death. He took off his nightcap.

'I have come, sir, to ask your pardon for not ignoring a mere bagatelle to which, had I been wiser, I would have paid no attention. I have come to say that I have been more honoured than offended by you, and to ask for your protection in the future against your friends who, since they do not understand your mind, think that they ought to be my enemies.'

'I admit,' he replied, 'that I insulted you, but you must admit too that I have paid dearly for it with my body. As for my friends, I shall declare myself the enemy of all those who do not treat you with respect. Biszewski has been degraded and banished, and that was well done. As for my protection, you have no need of it, because the King has as much esteem for you as I do, and as do all those who know the laws of honour. Sit down, and let us be good friends in the future. Bring this gentleman a cup of chocolate. So, you are quite healed?'

'Completely, apart for the articulation of the joint, which will take me a year to recover.'

'You fought well against the surgeons, and you were right when you said that those fools wanted to get into my good books by making you one-handed. They judged other people's minds by their own. I congratulate you on crushing them and keeping your hand. But I have never been able to understand how my ball could hit your hand after wounding you in the stomach.'

At this moment my chocolate was brought in, and the Grand Chamberlain entered, smiling at me. In five or six minutes the room was full of ladies and gentlemen who, having heard that I was with Branicki, and being curious to know what we said to each other, had come to find out. I could see that they had not expected to find us so friendly, and they were delighted by this. Branicki brought me back to the subject.

'How could my ball enter your hand?'

'If you allow me to take up the same position...'

'Please do so.'

I got up, and when I showed him how I had stood, he grasped it all.

One lady said to me, 'You should have kept your hand behind your body.'

'I was thinking rather, madame, of keeping my body behind my hand.'

'You tried to kill my brother, because you aimed at his head.'

'God forbid, madame. It was in my interest to keep him alive, so that he could defend me, as he has done, against his companions.'

'But you told him that you would aim at his head.'

'That's what one always says. But the wise man fires at the trunk, and the head is on its borders. It is true too that, as I raised the muzzle of my pistol, I stopped before it was quite horizontal.'

'That is true,' said Branicki. 'Your tactics were better than mine, and you taught me a lesson.'

'The lesson in heroism and sang-froid which Your Excellency gave me is much more worthy to be followed.'

'I think,' said his same sister, Sapieha, 'that you must have practised a great deal with the pistol.'

'Never in my life. This was my first unfortunate incident. But I have always had a good idea of what a straight line is, my eyes are keen, and my wrist does not tremble.'

'That's all that's needed,' said Branicki. 'And I have all that, and I am delighted that I did not shoot as well as I usually do.'

'Your ball, sir, broke the first bone of my finger. Here is the ball, as my bone flattened it. Allow me to give it back.'

'I am sorry that I cannot give you yours back.'

'Your wound seems to be better than I was led to believe.'

'There is some difficulty in getting a scar to form over my

wound. If I had done that day what you did, then this duel would have cost me my life. I am told that you dined very well.'

'The reason for that was that I was afraid that dinner was my last.'

'If I had dined, your ball would have pierced my intestines. Since they were empty, it passed above them.'

One thing that I knew for certain was that Branicki, as soon as he was certain that he was going to fight at three o'clock, went to Mass, made his confession, and took communion. So his confessor must have absolved him after he had said that his honour was obliging him to fight. That is still the ancient way of chivalry. For myself, more or less a Christian as Branicki is, I merely said a few words to God: 'Lord, if my enemy kills me, I shall be damned. So please preserve me from death.'

After we had exchanged a few more cheerful and pleasant words, I took my leave of the hero, and went to see the Grand Marshal to the Crown Bielinski (his sister is the Countess of Salmour). He is in his nineties and, because of his office, he is in complete charge of the administration of justice in Poland. I had never spoken with him. But he had defended me from Branicki's ulans, and since I owed him my life, I had to go and kiss his hand.

I had myself announced, I went in, and he asked me what I wanted of him.

'I have come to kiss the hand which has signed my pardon, sir, and I promise Your Excellency that I shall be wiser in future.'

'I advise you to do that. But as for your pardon, you should thank the King, for if he had not asked for it for you, I should have had your head struck off.'

'Despite the circumstances, sir?'

'What circumstances? Did you or did you not fight a duel?'

'That is not true. I fought only because I was obliged to defend myself. One could say that I fought a duel if Count Branicki had taken me out of the jurisdiction, as my first letter to him suggested, and as we had agreed. This is why I believe that, if Your Excellency had been well-informed, you would not have cut off my head.'

'I don't know what I would have done. The King wanted me to pardon you, which is an indication that he thought you deserved it, and I compliment you on that. I should be pleased if you would come and dine with me tomorrow.'

'I shall obey, sir.'

This old man was very renowned, and he had a good mind. He had been a great friend of the famous Poniatowski, the King's father. The next day at table he spoke much of him to me.

'What a consolation it must have been for Your Excellency's worthy friend,' I said, 'to see the crown on the head of his son.'

'He did not wish it.'

The force behind that reply allowed me to see into his soul. He was of the Saxon party.

On the same day I dined with the Prince Palatine who told me that reasons of State had prevented his coming to see me in the convent, but that I should not, because of that, doubt his friendship, for he had had me in mind.

'I am having an apartment prepared for you in my home,' he told me. 'My wife enjoys your company. But it will be six weeks before it is ready.'

'I shall spend that time, sir, in paying a visit to the Palatine of Kiovie, who has done me the honour of inviting me.'

'Who brought the invitation from him?'

'Count von Brühl, who is in Dresden, whose wife is the Palatine's daughter.'

'You do well to undertake that little journey at the moment, for this duel has made you a host of enemies, who are looking for a chance to pick a quarrel with you, and God preserve you from fighting again. Be on your guard, and never go out on foot, especially at night.'

For a fortnight I was invited to dinners and suppers, and everyone wanted to hear me tell the story of the duel in all its details. The King was often present, and he always made a pretence of not hearing; but he could not stop himself on one occasion from asking me if – supposing I had been insulted at home in Venice by a Venetian nobleman – I would have called the offender out.

'No, sir, because I would have realised that he would not respond.'

'What would you have done then?'

'I would have swallowed the insult. But if the same noble Venetian had dared to insult me in a foreign land, he would have given me satisfaction.'

When I visited Count Moscynski, I found Madame Binetti there, who made off when I appeared.

'What has she got against me?' I asked Moscynski.

'She was the reason for the duel, and you are the reason why she has lost her friend, for Branicki does not want to know her any more. She hoped he would treat you as he did Tomatis, and you almost killed her champion. She condemns him openly for accepting your challenge, but he will never see her again.'

Count Moscynski was as pleasant as it was possible for anyone to be; he had more than wit to recommend him. But he was generous to point of prodigality, and he ruined himself at Court by the presents he gave. His wounds were beginning to heal. The person who should have become more attached to me was Tomatis, but on the contrary he never welcomed me with the same pleasure as he had before my duel. He saw me as a silent reproach to his cowardice and his preference for money above honour. He might well have preferred it if Branicki had killed me, for then the author of his dishonour would have become the most hated man in Poland. And then perhaps Tomatis would have been more readily pardoned for the easy way in which he continued to be seen in the great houses, with all the fine company which he frequented and which fêted him, despite the stain which made him so despicable. It was obvious that all the favour he enjoyed came to him from the fanaticism which Madame Gattai aroused, more by her beauty and her sweet and modest manners than by her talent.

Determined to pay a visit to the malcontents who had recognised the new King only because they had to (and some of whom had not even been willing then to recognise him), I left with Campioni (because I wished to have a courageous friend with me) and one servant. I had two hundred sequins in my purse, a hundred of which had been given to me in private by the Palatine of Russia, in such a noble manner that I would have been very wrong to refuse them. I had won the other hundred by taking part in a game of quinze which Count Clary played against a Lord Sniatinski, who was happy to ruin himself in Warsaw. Count Clary who, between ourselves, never lost, won two thousand ducats that day, which the young man paid to him the next day. Prince Charles of Courland had left for Venice, where I had recommended him to my powerful friends, who gave him reason to be pleased. The Anglican minister who had recommended me to Prince Adam had arrived in Warsaw from St Petersburg. I dined with him at the home of the Prince himself. The King, who knew him, was there too. On that occasion we spoke of Madame Geoffrin, an old friend of the King who was coming to Warsaw, invited and paid for by the King himself who, despite the trouble which his enemies stirred up for him all the time, was always the life and soul of any company which he honoured with his presence. He told me one day, when I came upon him looking sad and thoughtful, that the crown of Poland was a martyr's crown. This King however, to whom I render all the justice that is his due, was weak enough to allow calumny to prevent his making my fortune. I have had the pleasure of convincing him that he was wrong. I shall speak about this shortly.

I arrived at Leopol six days after my departure from Warsaw, because I stayed for two days with the young Count Zamoyski, Lord of Zamosc, who had an income of forty thousand ducats, and who suffered from epileptic fits. He told me that he was ready to give all his wealth to the doctor who could give him back his health. I was sorry for his young wife. She loved him, and she did not dare to sleep with him, for he loved her, and his malady struck precisely when he wished to give her signs of his affection. She was in despair at having to refuse his overtures, and even make off, when he took it into his head to insist. This lord, who died shortly afterwards, lodged me in a fine apartment where there was nothing at all. That is the way in Poland, where they think that a gentleman travels with everything he needs.

I stayed at an inn in Leopol, which is also known as Lemberg; but I had to leave there to stay with the famous castellan, Kaminska, a great enemy of Branicki, of the King, and of all the King's party. She was very rich, but she has been ruined by faction. She entertained me for eight days, but without pleasure on either side, because she only spoke Polish and German. From Leopol I went on to a little village, whose name I forget, the home of the little general Joseph Rzewuski, to whom I brought a letter from Prince Lubomirski. He was a sturdy old man, and he had a long beard which he wore to indicate to his friends the sadness he felt at the innovations which disturbed his homeland. He was rich, learned, and superstitiously Christian, and urbane to excess. I stayed three days with him. As you would expect, he commanded the little stronghold where he lived, and where he had a garrison of five hundred men. The first day I lodged with him, I was in his room with three or four officers one hour before midday. As I was having an interesting conversation with him, an officer entered, approached him, and said a word in his ear. Then the same officer said in my ear: '*Venice and St Mark.*'

I replied out loud that St Mark was the patron saint of Venice. Then they all started to laugh, and I realised that this was the password for the day, and that I had been given it as a mark of honour. I begged pardon, and the subject was immediately changed. This lord talked a great deal about politics. He had never been to Court, but he had decided to attend the Diet to oppose strongly the Russian laws which favoured the dissidents. He was one of the four whom Prince Repnin later had arrested and sent to Siberia.

After taking my leave of this great republican, I went to Krystynopol, the home of the famous Palatine of Kiovie, Potocki, who had been one of the lovers of the Empress of Russia, Anna Ivanovna. He had himself built the town where he lived, and had called it Krystynopol after his own name. This lord, who was still handsome, maintained a magnificent court. He honoured Count von Brühl's request to the letter, keeping me with him for a fortnight, and making me pay a visit every day to his doctor, who was the celebrated Hyrneus, sworn enemy of the even more celebrated Van Swieten. This Hyrneus, who was very learned, was also rather foolish; he was a quack, and followed Aesculapius' system, which has become untenable after the great Boerhaave; but despite all that, he effected amazing cures. Every evening, on returning to Krystynopol, I paid my respects to Madame the Palatine, who never came down to supper since the devotions she exercised in her room did not permit it. I never saw her without her three daughters and two Franciscan friars who took turns to direct her conscience.

At Leopol I amused myself for a week with a very beautiful girl who shortly afterwards made Count Potocki, Lord of Sniatyn, fall so deeply in love with her that he married her.

After Leopol, I stayed for a week in Pulawi, a superb palace on the Vistula eighteen leagues from Warsaw, which belonged to the Prince Palatine of Russia. He himself had had it built. There, Campioni left me to go to Warsaw. Any place at all, however boring, can always be charming for a man who is condemned to live there alone, provided he has some literary work in hand.

In Pulawi I took a liking to a peasant girl who came into my room, and one morning she fled away, shouting out that I had tried to do something to her. The doorkeeper ran up, and asked me coldly why I did not act in a more direct way if I liked the girl.

'What is the direct way?'

'Speak to her father, who is here, and ask him politely if he is willing to sell you her virginity.'

'I do not speak Polish. Arrange this matter yourself.'

'With pleasure. Will you give him fifty florins?'

'You are joking. If she is a virgin, and as meek as a lamb, I shall give him a hundred.'

The matter was concluded the same day after supper. Afterwards, she made off like a thief. I heard that her father had been obliged to beat her to make her obey. The next day I was offered several others without even being allowed to see them.

'But where is this girl?' I asked the doorkeeper.

'Why do you need to look her in the face when you are assured that she is a virgin?'

'Take note that what I am interested in is the face, and that taking the virginity of an ugly girl is a drudgery for someone of my strange tastes.'

They then began to let me see them, and on the eve of my departure I was accommodated with another. In general, the women in that country are ugly.

I left for Warsaw. And so I saw Podolia, Pokucie, and Volhynia, which a few years later were known as Galicia and Lodomerien, for they could not belong to the House of Austria without changing their names. They do say, however, that these fertile provinces are happier now they are no longer Polish. At the present time Poland is no more.

In Warsaw I found Madame Geoffrin, who was being fêted everywhere, and who astonished everyone who saw her by the simplicity of her dress.

I found that I was not only received very coldly by everyone, but positively ill-received.

'We did not expect,' someone said to me bluntly, 'to see you again in this country. Why have you come here?'

'To pay my debts.'

I found all that disgusting. Even the Palatine of Russia seemed to have become a different person. I was received at tables where I had been accustomed to go, but no one spoke to me. However, the Princess who was the sister of Prince Adam invited me kindly to take supper with her. I went there, and at a round table I found myself face to face with the King, who did not address one single word to me. He did not speak except to the Swiss, Bertrand. That had never happened to me before.

The next day I went to dine with Countess Oginska, daughter of Prince Czartoryski, Grand Chancellor of Lithuania, and of a Countess of Waldstein, a person most worthy of respect, who lived to the age of ninety. At table this lady asked where the King had supped the evening before. No one knew, and I kept silent. General Ronikier arrived as we were leaving the table. The Palatine asked him where the King had supped, and he said that he had supped with Princess Strasnikowa, and that I too had been there. She asked me why I had said nothing at table when she had shown herself to be curious. I answered that this was because I was annoyed to be there and find that the King said not a word to me, or even looked at me.

'I am in disgrace, and I cannot find out the reason.'

On leaving the Palatine of Vilna, Oginski, I went to pay my respects to that wise man, Prince August Sulkowski, who, after welcoming me heartily, as he always did, told me that I had made a mistake in returning to Warsaw, because everyone there had changed their minds about me.

'What have I done?'

'Nothing. But that's the way we are: inconstant, inconsistent, awkward. *Sarmatarum virtus veluti extra ipsos.*[4] Your fortune was made, but you lost your chance. I advise you to go away.'

'Then I shall go away.'

I went home, and at six o'clock my servant gave me a letter which had been left at my door. I opened it. There was no signature. Someone who liked me and respected me, and who did not sign the letter because he had had the information from the King himself, was warning me that the King did not wish to see me at Court any more. The King had been told that I had been hanged in effigy in Paris for taking with me, when I left, a very large sum of money from the coffers of the lottery of the Military School. He had also been told that in Italy I had been employed in a menial position – as a strolling player.

Such are calumnies: very easy to spread, and very hard to silence. Such are courts, where hatred is always at work, aroused by envy. I wished I could have scorned them and departed immediately, but I had debts to pay, and not enough money to get to Portugal where I was certain of great resources.

I stopped going anywhere. I saw no one but Campioni. I wrote to Venice, and to anywhere where I had friends, to try to get some funds. Then the same lieutenant-general who had been present at my duel came to me, looking sad. He came to tell me in the name of the King that I must leave the jurisdiction of Warsaw within a week. I bridled at this, and told him to tell the King that I did not feel disposed to obey such an order.

'If I have to go,' I told him, 'I want everyone to know that it is under compulsion.'

'I will not undertake to deliver that reply. I shall tell the King that I have carried out his order, and no more. You will do whatever you think fit.'

In my exasperation, I wrote the King a long letter. I pointed out to him that honour obliged me to disobey his orders. 'My creditors, Your Majesty, will pardon me when they know that I have left Poland without paying them simply because I was forced to leave.'

I wondered who could deliver this letter for me. Then Count Moscynski visited me. I told him all that had happened, and after he had read my letter, I asked him who I might ask to deliver it. He replied with feeling that he would do so himself. Then I went out to take a little air, and I came across Prince Sulkowski, who was not surprised to learn that I had been ordered to leave.

Then that Prince told me in detail all that had happened to him in Vienna, where the Empress Maria Theresa had caused him to be notified that he must leave the Court within the space of twenty-four hours, for no other reason than that he had paid his respects to the Archduchess Christine on behalf of Prince Louis of Württemberg.

The next morning the Stolnik to the Crown, Count Moscynski, came and brought me a thousand ducats. He said that the King did not know that I needed money, that I had much more need to preserve my life, and that it was for this reason that His Majesty had sent me the order to leave: if I remained in Warsaw, and went out at night, I would always be in great danger. This danger derived from five or six people who had written to me, but to whom I had not even replied. These people might attack me to take revenge on me for my scorn, and the King did not wish to be uneasy on my account. He said further that the King's order was no dishonour to me: one must bear in mind the person who had brought it, the circumstances, and the time allowed to me which meant that I could leave at my convenience. The result of this conversation was that not only did I give my word to Count Moscynski to depart, but I also begged him to thank His Majesty on my behalf for the favour he was showing me, and for the indication he was giving me of concern for my life.

Moscynski embraced me, and generously begged me to

accept the small present of a carriage, since I did not have one, and he begged me to write. He told me that Madame Binetti's husband had gone off with his wife's chambermaid, with whom he had fallen in love, taking with him all her diamonds, her watches, her golden snuffboxes, and as many as thirty-six sets of golden cutlery. He had left with the dancer Piq, with whom she was sleeping every night. Binetti's patrons, of whom the Prince General, the King's brother, was the main one, had united to console her and had given her enough to make up for what her scoundrel of a husband had stolen. He told me that the King's sister, the wife of the Grand General to the Crown, had arrived from Bialystok, and that she was living at the Court, where she was treated with the greatest of honour. There were hopes that her husband would eventually decide to come to Warsaw. He was that Count Branicki who died, saying that he was the last of his line, and commanding, as was the custom, that his arms should be buried with him. The Branicki who honoured me with a duel was not related to him, but had misappropriated the other's name: his real name was Branecki[5].

The next day I paid my debts, which amounted to two hundred ducats, and I got ready to leave the next day but one for Breslau with Count Clary. He went in his carriage, and I went in mine which Count Moscynski had sent to me. Count Clary left without ever having been at Court. That did not trouble him, for he did not care for good company or decent women, being interested only in gamblers and whores. He had arrived in Warsaw with Madame Durand, a dancer whom he had brought from Stuttgart where she had been in the Duke's service. This had displeased the Duke, who was not much inclined to be tolerant. In Warsaw Clary had grown tired of Madame Durand, and had got rid of her by sending her to Strasbourg. And so he left alone, as I did, with just one servant. He told me that he would leave me in Breslau, because he wanted to go to Olomouc to visit his brother who was a canon there. He made me laugh when he told me of his affairs without being asked, for in everything he said there was not a word of truth. I have known three men of quality who had this low vice. Those who have it are to be pitied. They are in the difficult position of not being able to tell anyone the truth any more, when it is in their interest that those who listen to them should believe them. This Count Clary, who was not of the Clary family of Toeplitz, could neither go back to his own country nor to Vienna, because he had deserted on the eve of a battle. He was lame, but no one knew this, because his lameness did not appear when he walked. That was the only truth which he could hide without wronging anyone. He died in Venice in poverty. I shall speak of him in eleven or twelve years. He was a handsome man, with a pleasant and prepossessing face.

We got to Breslau, travelling day and night, without anything untoward happening. Campioni had gone some way with me, accompanying me as far as Wartemberg. There he had left me to return to Warsaw, where he had a romantic attachment. He rejoined me in Vienna seven months later; I shall speak of that in its place. Failing to find Baron Treyden in Wartemberg, I only stayed there two hours. When Count Clary left Breslau at dawn the next day, it occurred to me, as soon as I was alone, to make the acquaintance of Abbot Bastiani, a celebrated Venetian, who had made his fortune with the King of Prussia. He was the cathedral canon.

He welcomed me as I wished, cordially and straight-forwardly. We were both equally curious about each other. He was fair, with a good figure, well-shaped, and six feet tall; he had a good mind, a good knowledge of literature, a persuasive eloquence, a characteristic gaiety, a good library, a good cook, and a good cellar. He was well accommodated on the ground floor. On the first floor he had a lodger, a lady of whose children he was very fond, perhaps because he was their father. He was a lover of the fair sex, but not exclusively so: from time to time he fell in love with a young man, and he yearned to make a conquest of him in the Greek way, but found obstacles in his way that were the result of education, prejudice, and what are known as morals. This passion of his was very much in evidence during the three days I spent in Breslau, dining and having supper with him every day. He longed for the young Abbot Count Cavalcabo. He never took his eyes off him. He swore to me that he had not yet got as far as a declaration, and that perhaps he never would, for fear of exposing himself to the risk of compromising his dignity. He showed me all the love-letters which he had received from the King of Prussia before he became a canon. This monarch had been deeply in love with Bastiani, he wanted to become his 'mistress', and he rewarded him, as King, by giving him an ecclesiastical honour. This abbot was the son of a Venetian tailor, he had become a Franciscan friar, and he had escaped from tyrannical persecution. Having escaped to La Haye, he found there the Venetian ambassador, Tron, who lent him a hundred ducats, and he went to Berlin, where the great Frederick found him worthy of his love. It is by ways like this that men often make their fortune. *Sequere Deum.*[6]

The day before my departure, at eleven o'clock in the morning, I visited a baroness to deliver a letter from her son who was in the service of the King in Warsaw. I had myself announced, and I was asked to wait for half an hour to give the lady time to dress. I sat down on a sofa by the side of a young girl, who was pretty and well-dressed, with a tippet and a work-bag. She interested me, and I asked her if she also was there to speak to the baroness.

'Yes, sir. I have come to offer my services to Madame as French governess to her three young daughters.'

'A governess at your age?'

'Alas! Age has nothing to do with it when one is in need. I have lost my father and mother, my brother is a poor lieutenant who can give me no assistance. What do you expect me to do? I can only live honestly by turning the little education which I have had to some account.'

'And what will you earn as a governess?'

'Alas! Fifty wretched écus to buy myself clothes.'

'That is very little.'

'They don't give any more.'

'And where are you living at present?'

'With a poor aunt, where I make a living by sewing shirts the whole day.'

'If, instead of becoming a children's governess, you would like to become governess to a man of honour, come and live with me. I will give you fifty écus, not per year, but per month.'

'To be your governess? Governess to your family, you mean?'

'I have no family, I am alone, and I travel. I am leaving tomorrow morning at five o'clock for Dresden, alone in my carriage, where there will be a place for you if you wish. I am staying at *** hotel. Come with your luggage before I leave, and we shall be off.'

'You're joking! And besides, I don't know you.'

'I am not joking, and as for knowing me, I ask you which of the two of us has more reasons for getting to know the other. We shall know each other perfectly well within twenty-four hours, and there is no more to it than that.'

The serious tone in which I spoke and my air of candour convinced the girl that I was not joking; but she was very astonished. For my part I was surprised that I had made seriously a proposal which I had only broached in order to say something pleasant. In trying to persuade the girl, I had persuaded myself. My action seemed to me to be, by every sensible way of looking at it, a blunder; but I was pleased to see that she was thinking about it, for every now and then she cast her eyes on me to see if I was making fun of her. I fancied that I knew the thoughts that were occupying her mind, and I interpreted everything to her advantage. This was a girl whom I was going to bring into the light of day, and whom I was going to educate in the ways of the great world. I did not doubt her wisdom or her feelings, and I congratulated myself on my good fortune, since I was about to enlighten her by destroying the false notions of virtue which she had. In my infatuation, I drew two ducats from my pocket, and I gave them to her as an advance for the first month.

The baroness appeared, she read the letter twice, asked fifty questions about her son, asked me to dinner the next day, and she was mortified when I told her that I was leaving at dawn the next day. I thanked her, however, took my leave of her, and I went back to Bastiani without even noticing, when I came out of the baroness' room, that the young girl was no longer where I had left her.

I dined with the abbot, we spent the whole day playing ombre, we supped well, and then we embraced and said goodbye. Early the next day, everything was ready, the horses were harnessed, and I departed. A hundred yards from the gate, the postilion stopped. The window at my right was lowered, and a parcel came through. I looked up and I saw the young lady, whom to tell the truth I had not remembered. My servant opened the door for her, she sat by me; I thought it was all accomplished marvellously, I praised her, swearing that I had not expected such spirit, and we went off. She told me that she had warned the postilion a quarter of an hour before that he must stop when he saw her, and that this was on my orders.

'You are very well organised, for God knows what they would have said at the inn. They might have prevented you from going.'

'Oh, that is no problem. Even in Breslau they will not know that I have left with you unless the postilion tells them. However, I would not have made up my mind to come if you had not given me the two ducats. I did not wish to give you occasion to say that I was dishonest.'

NOTES

1. Leopol is the modern Ukrainian city of Lviv (known in Polish as Lwow, and German as Lemberg).
2. Outside a theatre, Branicki had taken Tomatis' place in his carriage and, in the ensuing quarrel, had ordered one of his attendants to give Tomatis a box on the ear. Tomatis was a friend of Casanova.
3. Modern Vilnius.
4. The courage of the Sarmatians is, so to speak, external to themselves.
5. In fact, Branicki's real family name was Korczak.
6. Follow God.

Giacomo Casanova was born in Venice in 1725, the son of Gaetano Casanova, an actor and director. A sickly child, Casanova was not expected to live long, and was left in the care of his grandmother whilst his parents travelled to London. At the age of nine, he was sent to a seminary in Padua but was later expelled for his decadent lifestyle. Turning his back on a life in the Church, he entered the Army, but his time there too proved shortlived, and he embarked upon a nomadic life as a violist, playwright and translator.

In 1755 Casanova was arrested on a charge of being a magician. After only a year of his five-year sentence he escaped from gaol, fleeing first to Paris where he made the acquaintance of Louis XV, and then to Naples, England, Germany, Spain, and latterly to Prague. Working undercover as a spy, Casanova here continued his literary career with translations (including Voltaire) and historical narratives. His work however was largely unsuccessful.

In the last years of his life, he composed his memoirs – partly to relieve his increasing boredom and partly to leave a record of his remarkable adventures. The result was his vast *Histoire de ma vie* – a colourful picture of eighteenth-century life and a true proof of Casanova's literary skill. The work was completed shortly before his death in 1798, although it was not published until some years later.

J.G. Nichols is a poet and translator. His published translations include the poems of Guido Gozzano (for which he was awarded the John Florio prize), Gabriele D'Annunzio, Giacomo Leopardi and Petrarch (for which he won the Monselice Prize).

HESPERUS PRESS – 100 PAGES

Hesperus Press, as suggested by the Latin motto, is committed to bringing near what is far – far both in space and time. Works written by the greatest authors, and unjustly neglected or simply little known in the English-speaking world, are made accessible through new translations and a completely fresh editorial approach. Through these short classic works, each little more than 100 pages in length, the reader will be introduced to the greatest writers from all times and all cultures.

For more information on Hesperus Press, please visit our website: **www.hesperuspress.com**

SELECTED TITLES FROM HESPERUS PRESS

Gustave Flaubert *Memoirs of a Madman*
Alexander Pope *Scriblerus*
Ugo Foscolo *Last Letters of Jacopo Ortis*
Anton Chekhov *The Story of a Nobody*
Joseph von Eichendorff *Life of a Good-for-nothing*
Mark Twain *The Diary of Adam and Eve*
Giovanni Boccaccio *Life of Dante*
Victor Hugo *The Last Day of a Condemned Man*
Joseph Conrad *Heart of Darkness*
Edgar Allan Poe *Eureka*
Emile Zola *For a Night of Love*
Daniel Defoe *The King of Pirates*
Giacomo Leopardi *Thoughts*
Nikolai Gogol *The Squabble*
Franz Kafka *Metamorphosis*
Herman Melville *The Enchanted Isles*
Leonardo da Vinci *Prophecies*
Charles Baudelaire *On Wine and Hashish*
William Makepeace Thackeray *Rebecca and Rowena*

Wilkie Collins *Who Killed Zebedee?*
Théophile Gautier *The Jinx*
Charles Dickens *The Haunted House*
Luigi Pirandello *Loveless Love*
Fyodor Dostoevsky *Poor People*
E.T.A. Hoffmann *Mademoiselle de Scudéri*
Henry James *In the Cage*
Francis Petrarch *My Secret Book*
André Gide *Theseus*
D.H. Lawrence *The Fox*
Percy Bysshe Shelley *Zastrozzi*
Marquis de Sade *Incest*
Oscar Wilde *The Portrait of Mr W.H.*
Leo Tolstoy *Hadji Murat*
Friedrich von Schiller *The Ghost-seer*
Nathaniel Hawthorne *Rappaccini's Daughter*
Pietro Aretino *The School of Whoredom*
Honoré de Balzac *Colonel Chabert*
Thomas Hardy *Fellow-Townsmen*
Arthur Conan Doyle *The Tragedy of the Korosko*